BLESS THE MOTHER

L.C. MARINO

Also in The Haunting of the Whispering House Series

Available in paperback, eBook, and audiobook.

Bury the Child
Burn the Girls

CONTENTS

For Tammie.

I love you.

CHAPTER 1

ABIGAIL

February 16, 1986

The Whispering House loomed over Abigail in damning silence. Twenty years separated her from her life-altering final night in the house. Now, standing so close to the home felt like a full circle moment.

You've taken so much from us, she thought, opening her eyes to look up at the neglected white facade. Paint peeled at the hard edges of windows and eaves. A layer of wind-blown pollen and dirt coated every surface within sight.

I can't forgive you for the damage you've done to us. But I have to find answers to my questions.

Is my mother free of your damnation?

Is my dear cousin Adeline still suffering a horrible death every night?

Is Aunt Lydia blindly searching the rooms for Adeline? Is she still tormented by loss?

Or did you finally return them to their graves in the family cemetery?

This place had ruined them. Aunt Jenny, Uncle Hank, Constance, and Uncle Wade–they'd all suffered terribly, and all because of this house.

Why did you spare me?

Abigail had fared well, all things considered. She'd had a mostly normal life. She gained friendships and lost loved ones. After finishing high school, she worked a few retail jobs and eventually built a successful bookstore in town. Most importantly, she'd reciprocated the care and love that she'd once depended upon for survival. She provided strength to Aunt Jenny when Uncle Hank passed from a heart attack in his sleep in 1983. She cared for Aunt Jenny until a stroke took her as well two years later. Now, it was just Abigail and Constance in the small ranch style home in the woods near the York River.

But this house–it stayed with them. The trauma of their last night in the home had been so severe for their family that Aunt Jenny refused to let Abigail and Constance return to the property except for trips to the cemetery on their deceased mother's birthday and Christmas each year. Even in their adult years, the girls respected Aunt Jenny's wishes and avoided the slowly dying structure during their visits, sticking solely to the cemetery path. Constance shared Aunt Jenny's steadfast condemnation of the home. After Aunt Jenny passed, Constance begged Abigail to continue avoiding the place. And Abigail had honored her request.

Until today.

Now, only her will to walk up those softening wooden steps and through that door stood between Abigail and the answers she sought. Committing to the danger may bring her to the souls potentially waiting beyond the home's threshold.

Placing one hand on the side of the house for balance, she raised her right foot over the bottom step. Abigail closed her eyes and gently lowered her leg, settling into the moment. She listened intently with her ears, then her mind. She drew deep breaths and waited for images of her mother to flood her thoughts, but none came.

Are you there?

Nothing.

Abigail opened her eyes and scanned the porch windows. The sheer curtains hung perfectly still in the shade. The two rocking chairs that once sat between those windows were long gone, removed years ago after Uncle Hank moved them out of the house.

That's a good sign, she thought and relaxed her tense shoulders. She climbed the steps and approached the solid wood front door. She drew an old brass key from her right pocket and pressed it into the lock. The lock's tumblers protested, but eventually took the key in fits of resistance. Her fingers curled around the cool metal doorknob, and again, she closed her eyes and listened.

Please be here.

Abigail tottered on a narrow ledge between wanting silence and craving contact. Her mother appeared to her here once before. Perhaps she'd find her on the other side of the heavy door, beautiful in her waiting.

That's ridiculous. You were a child, and your imagination amplified your experience.

Over the years, she'd grown leary of her memories from that period. With each passing day, the reality of this house grew more scrambled and untrustworthy as time eroded the accuracy of her recollection.

There's no denying what happened. The evidence of the haunting coats every element of your life. For God's sake, look at what it did to your sister. You don't get more real than that.

Even so, her mind harbored doubts. Now faced with full ownership of the house and a decision to sell or keep the property, she needed confirmation. She wanted to know the truth before she sold their inheritance, their *legacy*, to some stranger.

Remember what Aunt Jenny said. This house is tainted. You can never live here again.

But if it wasn't safe for her and Constance, how could it be safe for anyone? How could she sell it in good conscience?

And if it was safe for someone else, why couldn't it be safe for them?

Abigail drew a shaky breath, took one brief glance over her shoulder to the empty yard behind her, and entered the Whispering House.

CHAPTER 2

CONSTANCE

Constance sat at her large desk in the back office of The Poisoned Page bookstore. A casual observer would hardly agree the space was tidy, but it was just how Constance needed it. She craved order and couldn't stand when things weren't where they should be. The space had enough clutter as it was. Books towered in precarious columns amid strategically placed stacks of paper on nearly every flat surface. A small gray Radio Shack AM/FM radio tuned to WNOR 98.7 played "You Got Lucky" from Tom Petty and the Heartbreakers. She got decent reception on most days as long as no one moved her antenna.

Everything in its right place.

A document sat open on her new Commodore Amiga 1000 desktop computer. It was the most expensive thing she owned other than her car. Abigail had given her the new machine for Christmas under the guise of a mutual business investment. Constance could use it to boost her writing career and manage the store's paperwork. She had initially been hesitant to migrate from her Smith-Corona electric typewriter, but she'd quickly grown to appreciate the benefit of a computer for corrections and saving money on paper. Her latest manuscript, yet to be named but most definitely ready to be, stared at her from the 13-inch monitor sitting atop the rectangular machine. To the right, her gray 3.5 inch floppy disk sat in its doc, carrying weeks of progress from her WordPerfect 2.0 word processor.

I'll die if anything happens to that little disk, she thought.

New Blood on Old Soil, the third book in her series, filled the floppy disk with her last four months of work. She sat back in her worn leather desk chair and exhaled in relief as the dot matrix printer beside her whirred and buzzed its rhythmic mechanical tune. The pages of her latest chapter fed out of the machine in one long, connected ream of paper. She didn't need to print every chapter after she wrote, but she didn't completely trust the new technology yet. Sticking to the process she knew gave her a certain peace of mind.

Despite losing any semblance of normalcy twenty years ago in the fateful encounter in the home, Constance had realized one dream–she'd become a published author. She was a far cry from being a "successful author", whatever that was, but she'd published and gained some local notoriety in the region. Unfortunately, her love of writing also tethered her to the worst day of her life. She'd tried publishing several fantasy and science fiction stories at first, but she couldn't gain traction with readers or publishers. After years of failing to grab the attention of the industry, she took the advice of a few fellow authors in the Williamsburg Writers Club and wrote a paranormal horror story based on her experiences after her mother's tragic death in 1966.

Ironically, it worked. She finally found a modicum of success by writing about the worst experience in her life. The situation emotionally and physically crippled her. She'd always viewed writing as an escape from her harsh realities, a way to explore a broader landscape than the limitations of her small southern Virginia county. Writing also soothed her anxious, reactive tendencies. For many, writing about such a traumatic event would have proved cathartic. But not for Constance. She'd lost much of that therapeutic relief by continuously exploring the incident and circumstances which robbed her of her future. She relived the nightmare, the visions, the terror–for a living.

Constance snapped out of a daze as the printer's speed shifted to rapid fire. She leaned in her chair to inspect the paper streaming from the printer in jerky, robotic movements.

What the ...

The pages streamed from the tray, folding over on each other behind the out-feed. Each page bore the same text, over and over.

```
True love is deeper than any grave.
True love is deeper than any grave.
True love is deeper than any grave.
```

Constance squeezed her webbed, scarred eyes shut and whispered a calming chant.

It's not real, you're dreaming.

It's not real, you're dreaming.

It's not real, you're dreaming.

The printer stopped its robotic screaming. Constance repeated the mantra several more times, then slowly opened her eyes. The final paragraphs of her text played out across the last sheet sitting on the tray. Constance reached with shaking hands and lifted the previous pages from the running stream.

Everything looked fine. There was no sign of the troubling quote on any sheet of paper in the stack. Those words from her dead aunt had bounced around her mind for the past twenty years, but they ceased to actually exist here in the physical world.

Constance exhaled and dropped her head in relief. No matter how much time passed, she couldn't escape the physical and mental scars of that terrible day. Thankfully, the most vivid dreams and visions burned in the fire that tragically consumed her beauty at the young age of eighteen, leaving her with brief departures from reality.

Over the years, she'd learned to wait out the brief visions, thankful that none manifested as severely debilitating experiences like those she'd experienced before the confrontation in the sitting room. Those visions and dreams had been weapons of psychological warfare brandished by Aunt Lydia to separate Constance and Abigail. Now, she placed the blame squarely at the feet of her psychosis. Her visions were merely a prolonged effect of her trauma. Back then, she considered herself haunted. Now, she considered herself simply broken.

Needing some fresh air, Constance pushed her rolling chair away from the desk and stood. She stretched her lower back, the scars across her abdomen and hips protesting in sharp bolts of pain. She left the office and walked into the narrow hallway that connected the front of the bookstore to the offices and rear access. Pressing her bodyweight into the back door, she winced against the bright, clouded winter sky. She looked around the rear parking lot to make sure she was alone before propping the door open with a stray brick from the alley to prevent it from locking shut behind her. Constance blinked her eyes, clearing traces of the computer's monitor image from her mind. She suspected one day they'd discover that staring at a computer screen all day damages your vision and by then, it'd be too late for her.

Closing her eyes again, Constance rubbed her face with both hands as she yawned. Dropping her hands, she opened her eyes to the front yard of the Whispering House. Abigail stood on the other side of the yard at the base of the front porch steps.

Constance froze in sudden fear.

This can't be happening.

Her mind spun. Déjà vu set in *hard*.

I've seen this in a dream before–standing here in the yard, Abigail at the steps, but something is missing.

The front door opened, and her mother, Aunt Lydia, and Adeline emerged from the dark house to greet Abigail.

The memory blitzed her. Her mouth dropped as she recalled her last horrific dream in the hospital.

No, Abigail! Don't go with them.

She lifted her right foot to run to her sister and her body went rigid as if a puppeteer jerked her strings. Her panic boiled over as she realized she'd lost control of her body.

Abigail lifted her head and climbed the steps to the house. The dead welcoming committee parted to allow her passage to the door. After a brief pause, Abigail entered the home and the windows came alive with light. Mama, Aunt Lydia, and Adeline followed Abigail into the belly of the beast.

As the door slammed shut behind them, Constance stumbled forward mid-scream. She ran as fast as she could across the yard, clearing the stairs in two giant steps. She slammed hard into the front door. Constance grabbed the doorknob, but it refused to budge. Trying to get Abigail's attention, she punched and kicked the door in a desperate melee.

"Abi! Get out of there!"

Something moved in her peripheral vision. She turned from the door to the windows on the porch. Billowing smoke cast the sheer curtains into a smooth dance on the opposite side of the glass. Through the gap between the dancing curtains, she saw Abigail walk from the family room into the hall.

"Abi!" She beat the glass with her fists, but Abigail continued her slow saunter through the house, oblivious to the smoke or her sister's cries.

Constance fled the porch, hoping to find an open window around the side or back of the house. Reaching the back porch, she jumped over several pairs of muddy footprints crossing the open deck. She plowed through the screen door into the enclosed porch and grabbed the back doorknob, but it refused to turn. She peered through the door's glass window and saw Abigail walking back down the hall toward the front of the house.

"Abi! Get out, now!"

Constance raced back into the yard, scanning the windows for signs of movement. Light pulsed behind the glass but she couldn't see Abigail, or anyone else, inside. She ran back to the front yard. Smoke poured from the corners of the windows and eaves. The fire inside was growing fast.

Movement in the sitting room window caught her eye. The sheer curtains went up in a quick, consuming flame and fell from the curtain rod, giving a full view of the sitting room. Abigail stood before the fireplace, her face glowing in reflected flames.

Constance sprinted to the window, screaming her sister's name with her entire breath.

As she slammed into the glass pane, Abigail turned her head toward Constance.

Thank God she sees me.

Constance pulled her hands from the blistering hot window. She scanned the room, trying to determine if Abigail was alone. There was no sign of her mother, aunt, or cousin, but flames consumed every combustible surface in the room.

Abigail's calm face spread into an assuring smile. She raised one hand to her heart and spoke. Constance read her lips through the glass.

I'm sorry.

CHAPTER 3

CONSTANCE

Constance stood in front of the bookstore's bathroom sink, staring at herself in the mirror as she waited for the water to warm.

A disfigured creature stared back at her, still unfamiliar after all these years. The deformed skin looked like a hodgepodge of random depths, shades, and forms. Her narrow nose revealed too much nostril. Webbed lids hooded her once-bright eyes. Her plump lips lacked true symmetry with her mouth shut.

You ugly creature.

She'd been such a beautiful girl, and Constance often wondered what her life might have been like if not for the fire. Her throat tightened as tears threatened to spill from her eyes. The water running over her fingers lost its chill as the hot water finally reached the tap. She turned her cupped hands to the flow and rinsed the emerging emotion from her face.

Be careful closing your eyes again. You don't want another wild hallucination, do you?

"Shut up!" she said out loud to the empty bathroom.

She hadn't had an intense vision like that in nearly twenty years. However, she hadn't forgotten how vivid and real they felt. Her sister would most likely blame the incident on stress caused by compounding events. They'd recently lost Aunt Jenny to a stroke and now faced several important decisions, the biggest being what to do with the Whispering House.

Where the hell is Abigail? She should be here by now. She better not be at the house. She promised she'd steer clear of that place.

Constance dried her face and hands on a towel hanging on the wall to her left. She turned off the bathroom light, walked out of the door, and headed back to the main office. Before sitting down, she considered whether she should leave to find Abigail or stay and watch over the store. It wasn't like Abigail to be late, especially by two hours.

Constance knew she was overreacting. Abigail didn't need her searching for her like a missing person. But her vision behind the store worried her.

As if on cue, the bell over the front door chimed in the storefront.

Constance walked down the short hall and passed through a hanging curtain of beads to enter the space behind the checkout counter.

Abigail had the front door propped open with one foot, carrying a large box in both hands.

"I've got it." Abigail laughed and nearly dropped the box. She let out an exasperated sigh. "What a morning."

Constance crossed her arms. "I was getting ready to send out the search party. I wasn't sure where you were." She tried her best to hide her deep concern from showing in her voice.

"You're sweet. I'm sorry, I forgot to mention that I needed to stop on the way in today to renew our PO box and exchange packages."

Setting the heavy package on the counter, Abigail pulled her thick beanie hat from her head, her hair cast in all directions by static electricity from the friction.

"I wouldn't have been so concerned if it didn't take you so long. You never spend two hours at the post office."

Abigail's eyes shot to the clock hanging on the wall behind the counter. "Did it really take me that long? It didn't feel like it. They took forever finding the package in the back."

Abigail reached into the open shelves under the counter and pulled out a box cutter. She went to work on the tape binding the top of the package.

"You didn't stop by the house, did you?" The question came out before Constance could stop herself.

Abigail narrowed her eyes. "What house? Our house?"

Constance leaned forward to get Abigail's attention. "Don't play dumb. *The* house."

Abigail lifted a book from a sea of white foam peanuts in the box. "Oh, good! It's the new release of the *Encyclopedia Britannica*!"

"Are you listening to me? You didn't go to the house, did you?" Constance pressed one half of the box lid closed to get Abigail's attention and prevent her from lifting the next book.

Abigail sighed and looked her in the eyes. "I did."

"I knew it!"

"I only stopped by for a minute. I didn't tell you because I knew you'd get upset."

The world spun and Constance closed her eyes. She wanted to wring Abi's neck for not only going to the house, but lying about it.

Be careful, kid.

"Oh, shut the hell up!" Constance said out loud, but speaking to the voice in her head.

"Damn, Constance. I don't deserve that."

Constance exhaled in frustration and apologized. "I didn't mean *you*. I was talking to myself. Anyway, you aren't dodging this one. I told you not to go there and you promised me you wouldn't!"

Abigail looked down at her hands. "I'm sorry. One of us needs to figure out what to do with the place and I didn't want to upset you. I wouldn't dream of asking you to go into that house."

"I appreciate that, but it's not safe for either of us to be there. You know that better than anyone. What if something happened to you? No one knew you were there. I …" She stopped herself before she revealed her vision to Abigail.

"You what?"

Constance dodged her question. "I was worried about you. That's all."

Abigail leaned over the counter and looked directly into Constance's worried, scarred eyes. "I'm sorry. Okay? I won't go back alone."

Constance shook her head. "No, that's not good enough. Tell me you won't go back, *period*."

"I can't promise that, and you know it. If we sell the place, we'll need to do a walkthrough, fix things, and visit with the real estate agent. Come on. You know that's not fair."

"Promise me," Constance said sternly, tears building in her eyes.

Abigail must have seen how upset she'd made her. She huffed and dropped her shoulders.

"I promise."

CHAPTER 4

Abigail

Abigail sat in the waiting room of the law office, her thoughts occupied with the morning's events. Although she held a smidge of guilt about upsetting Constance, she also thought her visit to the house was necessary. Her sister's concerns were justified, no doubt. They had a uniquely tragic history in the home. However, they also had to make an informed decision about what to do with the property and Abigail didn't see how that was possible without being proactive. The house was the centerpiece of the only major decision to make after she resolved Aunt Jenny's will, which brought her to the Moeller and Moeller Law Offices that afternoon.

The aroma of vanilla and leather furniture permeated the office. Abigail smirked, thinking that's exactly what a law office should smell like.

The first meeting with the lawyer should prove a mere formality. Aunt Jenny and Uncle Hank had lived a fairly modest life, so Abigail expected a quick discussion about whatever funds remained in their bank accounts and the home they'd spent the past few decades in together.

She'd assumed correctly, and forty-five minutes after walking through the front doors, she left the law firm with a stack of papers in a fancy expanding binder to review, sign, and return.

Walking across the parking lot to her Honda Civic, Abigail considered running a few more errands before returning to the store. That's when she saw the sign for the Southern Charm Real Estate office on the opposite end of the lot, sitting in a line with other office suites. Abigail remembered her high school friend Glenda had worked there. They hadn't seen each other in a long time, and she thought it might be good to drop in and say hi. Maybe she could talk with her about the house. She walked past her car and headed for the office.

Once inside, a young secretary with a new wave hairstyle greeted her. The girl stood out against the traditional southern decor of the office. Glenda saw her through her office's open door and hurried out to greet her.

"Oh my God, girl! How *are* you?" Glenda squeezed Abigail in a tight, comforting hug, then held her at arm's length, her face beaming. Glenda was one of the nicest people Abigail had ever met. She'd maintained a radiant aura about her since they'd met in high school.

"I'm doing very well. Thanks for asking. How about you? Is the real estate game still fun?"

Glenda leaned back, lighting up with joy. "I *love* it! It keeps me busy and puts money in my bank account–two of my favorite things. Come on, let's talk in my office."

Abigail followed her into the office. Glenda shut the door behind her and gestured toward a set of inviting leather chairs flanking an ornate wooden coffee table.

"Would you like something to drink? I have Diet Rite, Dr. Pepper, and Canada Dry. Want one?"

"No, thank you. I'm trying to curb my soda intake."

"You're a stronger woman than me," Glenda said as she pulled a Diet Rite from a mini-fridge sitting against the wall. She pulled the can's tab, creating a distinct cracking sound as the aluminum seal broke. Abigail's stomach growled in protest.

"It's been so long since we've caught up." Glenda said. "It's funny how you can spend years growing up together and then life happens and you don't see each other anymore. How is the bookstore doing?"

"It's a wild ride. I spend my days emptying boxes and answering questions about books I'll never have the time to read. But I love it. It's clean, safe work except for the occasional paper cut. How is your mom doing?"

"She's good! She's getting up there in age, but she hasn't missed a step. Do you remember when you used to sleep over and we'd stay up to watch scary movies and she'd fall asleep and snore through the entire movie?"

"Those were the best sleepovers," Abigail said. "Then we hit high school and spent all our time studying in your room. We grew up too fast." The unspoken truth was the girls slowly drifted apart in high school. They never had a dramatic falling out, they simply moved on.

"Yeah, we sure did. Well, I'm sure you didn't come in just to reminisce. What's on your mind?" Glenda asked, leaning forward in her chair and placing her elbows on her thighs. She looked at Abigail with eager eyes, like the secret to eternal life would follow in her answer.

"Well, as you may know, my Aunt Jenny recently passed and I have several properties to manage now."

"I heard. I'm so sorry. She was the nicest lady."

"Thank you. She'd been sick for a little while and she's finally back with Uncle Hank now."

They let a necessary silence hold them for a moment before Abigail continued.

"So, now I have the house I've been living in with her for twenty or so years and the old family house and land on the other side of the county."

"Right," Glenda said with a knowing nod. There was no need to ask amplifying questions. Everyone their age in the county knew the rumors and lore about the Whispering House. "Are you looking to sell that place on Route 60?"

Abigail sighed. "I think so. I'm just not sure what condition it's in or where to begin with selling a house with such a ..." She knotted her fingers together, then released them. "... a reputation like it has. I mean, it's also sacred because our family cemetery's on the property."

"Right," Glenda said again, this time looking down into the small opening of her soda can. "Well, you have several options, including keeping the property, leveling the existing house, and building a custom home."

"I've considered that, but I can't afford to demo and build, even if I sold Aunt Jenny's place." She shook her head in frustration. "And I'm not sure living on that property is a good idea after what happened, so it's not really an option."

"That's understandable. Have you considered selling the portion of the land with the house on it and keeping the part with the cemetery?" Glenda asked.

"That may work if you think it wouldn't be weird," Abigail said.

Glenda relaxed in her chair and sipped her soda while she mulled over a response. "Honestly, that may be your best bet. You could easily sell a classic farmhouse like that to someone from out of town who isn't caught up in any local rumors about the place. And it's far less involved than relocating all the graves."

Abigail nodded. Constance would be relieved if they sold the house and kept access to the cemetery. They could make a new path to the cemetery on the land they kept. Maybe she could rent some of the remaining land to a local farmer as an investment property. Every dollar would help. The bookstore wasn't losing money, but it wasn't bringing in much profit either. She barely made ends meet, even without a mortgage on Aunt Jenny's old place.

Glenda stood. "I hate to cut this short, but I have an appointment with a potential buyer in ten minutes. Take a few days to think it over, then come by next week and let me know what you decide. I'm confident I can quickly sell it once we hit the market."

"Thanks," Abigail said. "I really appreciate your advice."

Now she only had to convince Constance she had a plan for the property.

CHAPTER 5

ABIGAIL

The late afternoon transitioned to dusk as Abigail and Constance drove home from the bookstore. Abigail tapped her fingers on the steering wheel to the opening notes of "Sweet Dreams" by The Eurythmics while she guided the Honda along the uncoiling road. She'd been waiting for the right moment to share her plan for the Whispering House with Constance. The opportunity presented itself at several points during the afternoon, but she hesitated each time, fearful of upsetting her sister or being interrupted by a customer. A dozen iterations of the conversation ran through her head since leaving Glenda's office. They all ended with Constance agreeing to sell the property. However, Abigail was nervous bringing it up because of the emotional response Constance had to *any* discussion about the house.

"So, how did your meeting go with the lawyer?" Constance asked.

That seemed like as good an offer as any to start the discussion. Keeping her eyes on the road, Abigail drew an anxious breath. "Quick and easy. I have a pile of paperwork to go through after dinner, but otherwise, this should be fairly effortless."

Go on, tell her about visiting Glenda.

"You know how those other businesses share the parking lot with them?" Abigail cringed at her awkward segue.

"Of course," Constance replied.

"Well, I had a few minutes to spare since the appointment ended so quickly, so I worked up the courage to walk into the real estate office across the lot."

"Where Glenda works?" Constance didn't seem bothered by this news.

"That's the one. She was there. We had a great conversation, and I think we've got a plan for the Whispering House."

"Why do you always do this?" Constance asked. "You act like I'm going to get upset, so you dance around the point. What did she say? What's the plan?"

"We'll sell it." She glanced at Constance, a slight smile lingering on her face.

"Really?"

"Really. And there's a way to do it so we can keep a good bit of the land and the family cemetery."

Neither of them spoke for a moment. Tremendous relief washed over Abigail now that she'd put this conversation behind them.

The approaching traffic light turned yellow, then red. As she eased the car to a standstill at the white line in the road, she noticed a woman with a massive flop of blonde hair and red-rimmed sunglasses in the next lane staring at them. Abigail met her gaze, raised her right hand as if to say, "Can I help you?", then returned to the setting sun dropping into the trees ahead as the woman looked away to avoid conflict.

"I hate people," Constance said without looking at the woman. "I'm the freak show that never ends. They just have to stare."

"That makes two of us," Abigail said, her good mood souring.

Green light. Gas pedal.

"So, what does this mean for us? Do we have to do anything to the house to get it on the market?" Constance asked.

"Well, it depends on how fast we want to sell it and how much money we want to make. The house needs a lot of love. It needs a good cleaning, a fresh coat of paint inside and out, tons of yard work, and all the systems checked. The furnace, electrical, plumbing, the chimney–all of it." She felt guilty for bringing up her visit.

"Well, can we sell it without doing all that? Would someone buy it as-is for a deal? We don't need to make a lot of money, we just need to get rid of it."

Butterflies fluttered in Abigail's chest. The stress of doing little and learning nothing about the spiritual remains of the house worried her. Working on the house may bring her closure after all these years. But she couldn't share that with Constance. The risk of being in the house seemed very different to Constance than it did to Abigail, despite her vivid memories and the obvious repercussions of that last night in the house. Abigail would take risks Constance wouldn't dream of.

And, of course, the money mattered more to Abigail than it did to Constance. Running a bookstore was hard enough, but getting customers into a store owned and operated by a social pariah made matters much worse. They sold enough books to pay the bills and buy necessities, but they were far from stable. The industry was naturally cyclical, with the busy season running through the fall and early winter. But sales slowed to a crawl when spring came and the sun lured people from their homes. Abigail could use some savings to give them breathing room during those down times.

"I'm not convinced it'll easily sell without some work on our part. Especially that far out of town."

"I'm not stupid," Constance said. "I know someone has to work on the place, but I don't want it to be us."

"We can't afford to hire people for everything. You know money is tight this time of year. Look, you don't have to do anything. But I'm comfortable being there and I can knock out the cleaning, interior painting, and yard work."

"What about the store? Who's going to man the counter while you're gone?" Constance's voice shimmered with emotion. She was too embarrassed by her appearance and her social anxiety to work the storefront alone. Abigail nodded knowingly. She'd expected this question.

"I'll close up for a few days. We can announce it ahead of time. It's not like we'll miss out on many sales at this time of year." Now she was getting emotional. Tremors radiated down her arms and into her hands, distracting her from the road. Constance must have noticed.

"Don't get upset. I'm sorry."

"It's okay. I just have a lot on my mind. I know we can handle this. It's a big project, but it's temporary. It may do me some good to get out of the store for a while."

Another stretch of silence settled on them. Abigail's mind naturally defaulted to obsessing over the details of the work list when Constance spoke up.

"You promised."

Abigail sighed, going silent. She *had* promised. But this was different. She'd promised not to visit the house alone. But she said nothing about working on the house.

"Come on. You know that's not fair."

"*You promised*," Constance doubled down.

Abigail exhaled in frustration. "I won't go alone. I'll coordinate my work with the other workers. Is that better?"

Constance turned and stared out of the window to avoid eye contact.

"You promised."

"I'm not twelve years old anymore. I'm a grown woman. I'll coordinate my work with the others and I'll be fine."

"Aunt Lydia was a grown woman, too."

Abigail glanced at her sister, her mouth agape. "That's not fair, and you know it! She wasn't right. Nothing about that situation was right. And we paid the price for getting close to it, I get it. But this isn't the—"

"Did we? Did *we* pay the price? One of us definitely did. *Look* at me."

"I'm not talking about this anymore." Abigail squeezed the wheel and pressed the gas pedal further. The faster they got home and out of this conversation, the better. Her fury turned from a sudden, unexpected surge into a simmering stew of decades-old anger. She'd spent two decades grieving the conflict in the house. Her words spilled from her without a filter.

"I was there, too, you know. *We* lost our mom. *We* lost our home. *I* saw you burn. I watched it all go down while our mother's ghost pinned me, helpless, to that goddamn couch. Lydia was *in* me. Her fire *burned in me* before it consumed you. Don't lecture me about her."

"Was that tough for you, Abi? Watching *me* burn?"

"Yes! I was terrified! I thought ..." she couldn't hold the tears back any longer. Disregarding the road and anyone behind them, she whipped the car onto an emerging side street. Loose books on the backseat slid into each other before spilling to the floorboard as the car stopped.

"I thought I'd lost you forever." Tears poured down her swollen face. She hid behind her shaking hands. "We can't do this. You're all I have. We need to stick together."

"That's *exactly* why I'm afraid, Abi. I'm terrified that if you go into that house, I'll lose you forever. I already sacrificed everything to protect you once."

Abigail lowered her hands and faced Constance. "You certainly did."

Her words hung in the stuffy car as Abigail eased the Honda back onto the main road. She'd never taken Constance's sacrifice for granted, and she'd spent the years since trying to return the favor. But now, they'd reached an impasse, and her need for closure and redemption far outweighed her concern for peace with Constance.

Promises be damned.

CHAPTER 6

ABIGAIL

The parking lot at Harry's buzzed with a flurry of commuters stopping on their way home from long days at work. Surprisingly, Abigail found an available parking spot close to the store's entrance.

"Lucky us," she said, trying to lighten the mood. She and Constance hadn't said a word to each other since their roadside argument, their silence a salve on the wound of disagreement. "I'll be quick. I'm just grabbing a frozen pizza."

"I'll hang here," Constance said, matter-of-factly. "Don't forget the half and half."

Abigail opened her door, locked the car, and reentered the cold outside world. She hurried around the car and across the parking lot in the biting wind. Winters in Virginia were unruly creatures. The damp air gave the cold temperatures teeth despite rarely bringing them snow. Lowering her head, she breached the grocery store entrance and welcomed a face full of warm air. Abigail grabbed a handbasket from a rack just inside and quickly headed for the refrigerated and frozen foods in the back aisles. She kept her head down as she maneuvered through the chip aisle, resisting the temptation to stock up on Jiffy Pop. Abigail hung a hard left at the end of the aisle and beelined for the frozen dinners. She'd been there a hundred times, reaching for the freezer door after a long day at the store. Each time, she desperately craved a hot shower and a few hours of senseless television to numb her brain with commercials and mediocre acting before dozing off on the couch.

"Excuse me."

Abigail stood like a statue in the open freezer door, staring blankly at the stacks of frozen pizzas. The woman's voice pulled her from her wandering thoughts.

"I'm sorry, I don't mean to interrupt," the forty-something woman with bloodshot eyes said. Abigail's brain skipped like a record.

How long have I been standing here holding this door open?

"Oh, I'm terribly sorry. I'll ... just ... sorry." Abigail quickly grabbed a pepperoni pizza from the shelf and held the door open for the woman.

"Thank you, but I don't need food," the woman said. She hesitated, then asked in a low voice, "Have you seen my little boy?"

"Um. No, I'm sorry I haven't." Abigail looked past the woman for the little boy, but they were alone. "Is he lost? Do you need me to help you look for him?"

The woman's eyes dropped to her fidgeting hands. "Well, sort of. I just figured maybe ... people say you can ...". Thick strands of brown hair streaked with wiry gray strays fell from the loose bun perched on her head and hung in her weary face. Her lips moved but made no sound. Finally, "I'm sorry. I shouldn't have interrupted you. Have a good night."

The woman rushed away; her wet boots squeaking on the tile floor with each departing step.

Abigail let the freezer door fall closed as the woman disappeared toward the registers. With the freezer door shut, the store's intense heat once again settled on her.

Clearing her head, she made her way to the checkout and paid for the pizza. She dropped her handbasket in the rack near the door and left the stuffy store for the frigid darkness of the new evening.

She stopped dead in her tracks as she stepped onto the sidewalk. Ten feet away, a small boy in a T-shirt and jeans with holes in the knees sat atop a change-operated children's ride under the piercing overhead lights. The mechanical rocket slowly passed back and forth through its hypnotic arc, carrying its passenger through every layer of the imaginary atmosphere between the earth's surface and the dreamy moon rising in the sky.

That kid's gotta be freezing, she thought as she punched her jacket around her neck to fend off the freezing wind. Head down, she hurried across the parking lot. As she approached the car, she saw Constance reading something in the passenger seat. Abigail unlocked the driver's side door and plopped into her seat. The car's interior wasn't much warmer than the outside, but the absence of wind made it feel balmy in comparison. She set the bag with the pizza on the rear floorboard behind them, started the car, and flipped on the heat. The headlights came alive and bathed the sidewalk at the store's entrance.

The boy looked in their direction. In the corner of her vision, Constance raised her head from her book.

"He must be freezing," Constance said. "Where's his mom?"

The front doors parted right on cue and the woman from the freezer aisle stepped into the Honda's headlights.

"I think that's her," Abigail said.

"Oh good," Constance went back to her book. The boy's mother looked toward the mechanical ride, now empty but still running through its programming. She looked back in their direction, this time shaking her head side-to-side as if denying some deeply disturbing reality. Her lips moved in the car's harsh lights.

Help me. Please.

Abigail choked back a groan, put the car in reverse, and backed out of her space. As they left the parking lot and pulled onto Route 60, Constance looked up from her book.

"You okay?"

"Yeah. I'm good."

A few minutes down the road, Constance glanced at the bag on the floorboard. "You forgot the half and half."

CHAPTER 7

ABIGAIL

Abigail woke the next morning feeling like she'd barely rested. She'd fallen asleep with no problems and didn't recall any bad dreams or waking moments, yet dragged like she'd been up all night. Still satiated from their late night dinner, she and Constance skipped breakfast, packed their lunches, and left for the bookstore as the sun's first rays met the horizon.

"Delaying coffee in the morning should be a misdemeanor." Abigail grumbled. She moved like a poorly programmed robot as she mindlessly drove their morning route to the bookstore. Her mind refused to come up to speed without her coffee.

"Well, someone forgot to get the creamer last night and refused to go back, so here we are."

"I was tired. Besides, we have plenty at the store. The coffee is just as good there as it is at home."

"But we didn't wake up at the bookstore. Did we? Now we wait and whither." Constance made an exaggerated fainting motion in the passenger seat. Abigail laughed.

"Stop being so dramatic. So, what's on your agenda today, Ms. Prolific Author?"

"Writing and more writing. I may get a little wild and read someone else's writing at some point."

Abigail smiled at the small joke. "Living dangerously, I see."

"What about you? Do you have any plans other than another riveting day of bookselling?"

Abigail bit her lip in hesitation, then went for it. "I'm going to swing by the industrial park this morning before we open and talk to some contractors about quotes for the house." She braced for resistance from Constance.

"That sounds good to me. Convince them to do everything."

"We'll see what they say. Maybe it won't be as expensive as I think to have them tackle the entire job."

"That would be great. But let's not discuss this any further until we've had coffee. I'm not responsible for my behavior until that happens," Constance yawned.

"Amen, sister."

Abigail leaned into the heavy glass door at TriCounty Construction a few minutes past eight. She left the frosty morning behind as she wiped her feet on the huge doormat lining the foyer floor. Outside, the building looked like an unassuming, bland brick box. However, the interior reflected the classic southern comfort Eli's business had become known for. Abigail admired the rich green and red colonial patterns on the oak furniture and window treatments and the ornate, stained wood molding wrapping the room. Although classic in its design, the place smelled like freshly applied sealants and paints. A custom, chest-high counter with a hand carved logo from a massive oak tree mounted to its face separated Abigail from the receptionist on the other side of the waiting room.

"Good morning. Welcome to TriCounty Construction," the receptionist droned without looking up.

"Good morning, Dee."

"Abigail Fairchild! I'm sorry, I didn't recognize you from behind this behemoth," Dee said as she stood to greet her. Standing helped little, as the counter was nearly as tall as the receptionist.

"No worries. Is Eli in? I need to bug him for a quote."

Dee's eyes widened. "Building a new house?"

"No, this is for a renovation."

"Wait, tell me you're renovating your aunt's place. I've always admired that house from afar. If only I could get my hands on it." Dee rubbed her hands together and hunched her shoulders like a greedy henchman in an old black and white film.

"Well, you'll have to wait until they drag me out of it in a body bag. We're not going anywhere."

Abigail's dark tone took the wind out of Dee's impression. Her smile disintegrated into a warped grimace.

"Right. Well, let me see if Eli is available." She leaned on one foot to see down the hall past the desk. "Eli! Abigail Fairchild is here to see you!"

Abigail winced as the woman's harsh voice cut through the air. What was the point of yelling down the hall when there was a phone within reach on the desk?

Eli appeared in his doorway at the end of the hall. The aggravated look on his face showed his disdain for Dee's approach.

"The phone, Dee. Use the phone. Come on back, Abi."

Dee shrugged her shoulders. "Go on back."

"Thanks." Abigail walked past the towering counter and down the narrow hall to Eli's office, passing a few closed doors along the way. He leaned in for a hug as she approached, and she happily obliged.

"Come on in and shut the door behind you."

"Gladly."

Eli's office kept the theme of the waiting area, but with a personal touch. His large mahogany desk sat in front of a substantial built-in. Pictures of his wife and three kids donned the shelves among several framed certificates, awards, and sports memorabilia. Eli had done exceptionally well for himself in the family department. Robin, his bombshell wife, won the title of Miss Jamestown in 1970, the year before they got married. Her brilliant blue eyes and relentless smile stole the breath from everyone she met. Their three lucky daughters looked like clones of their mother.

"Still cheering for the 'Skins? You know they suck, right?"

He laughed and rolled his eyes. "They aren't *that* bad. Wait. Do you even watch football?"

"Only when I have to. How is the family?" Abigail settled into a dangerously comfortable leather armchair across from his desk. "Gracious. You should let me take this chair home with me."

"Robin and the girls are great. It's remarkably difficult being the only man in a house of four women, but I'm getting by. I'm sure you didn't come here just to talk trash and steal my furniture."

"No. Unfortunately, I have some business to discuss. You know Aunt Jenny passed recently. Well, I've inherited the house."

Eli's smile slowly dripped from his face as he realized which house she referred to. "Oh."

"Yes. And I want to go through the house from top to bottom and make sure it's suitable for sale. Are you willing to help me?"

"Yeah, we'll take care of you and I won't charge a penny over the cost of materials," he said.

"I'm not asking for any favors. I just figured—"

"Not another word about it, Abi. I'll take care of it for you."

"Well, thank you." The words left her in a relieved sigh.

"It's cool if you don't know but, what condition is the interior in?"

His genuine question lay hidden in the trailing tone of his voice. *Is the fire damage bad?*

"I stopped in briefly yesterday. It looked a lot better than I expected. Honestly, I felt so guilty being there that I left in a hurry. I need to go back and really look the place over."

"I can't imagine going back there after all these years."
He looked at the pen flipping in his right hand to hide his
eyes from her.

"Look, I'll say this now and not bring it up again. I'll
understand if you change your mind about this project.
That was a brutal time in all our lives. I won't hold it
against you."

"No. I want to do this."

Abigail reached over the desk and took his hand in hers.
"Thank you, Eli."

He pressed his lips and nodded. "Want me to come
by the house with you? I can't go today, but Wednesday
works."

She considered his offer. "I'll take you up on that.
Wednesday. Eight o'clock?"

"In the morning?" He acted shocked.

"Smart ass. I'll meet you there."

"Sounds good."

Abigail turned and left his office with a tremendous
weight lifted from her shoulders. As she entered the narrow hall, she heard him exhale like a man holding his
breath under water.

CHAPTER 8

ABIGAIL

With her hands firmly on the steering wheel, Abigail stared at the Whispering House. The building stood in the overgrown lot like a tombstone in a poorly maintained cemetery.

"We already have one of those," she groaned as she emerged from her car in the driveway and walked the weed-choked path to the front steps. She'd planned to spend much more time talking with Eli about the project. Now she had time to kill before heading back to open the store. She figured it was wise to visit the house and start her to-do list before the craziness of the day stole her energy. Of course, she'd keep her visit to herself when she returned to the store to avoid another conflict with Constance.

She climbed the first porch step.

You promised. Constance's voice resonated in her ears as guilt wormed through her heart. She'd softened Constance's position since her visit to the house the day before, but she continued to sneak around behind her sister's back. Why?

She climbed the second step.

Because she'll never be okay with me being here. That's why.

As she continued climbing the stairs, the house presented itself like a devious gift–a forbidden experience, a familiar sin. Abigail welcomed the excitement in her otherwise boring life. She closed her eyes, her pulse quickening as she reached the porch.

So what if she chose a quick tryst with a potentially haunted house? Others chose adultery, addiction, and violent crime. She lived a clean, unassuming life.

"When you put it that way, you sound like a saint, girl."

She stood on the porch, staring at the paint peeling from the front door.

"I may as well start here." She opened her notepad and wrote, PAINT FRONT DOOR, in block letters at the top of a blank page. Then she lined through the words and wrote beside it, PAINT ENTIRE PORCH. "You'll end up painting the entire house before this is done and you know it." Her voice sunk into the soiled porch's damp wood surface. She pulled the key from her right front pocket and pressed it into the stubborn lock.

The door opened with the agonized screeching of dry hinges. Before crossing the threshold, she wrote in her notebook, OIL ALL DOOR HINGES. Closing her notepad, she stepped into the house, then stopped in the foyer.

Dense shadows and the scent of advancing mildew welcomed her inside, but she needed a moment to *listen* before she could trust the house.

A faint *tap tap tap tap* from the kitchen at the back of the house barely reached her in the foyer. She lifted her pad to note the potentially leaking kitchen faucet, then stopped. Why document the kitchen sink from here when she'd eventually reach the kitchen? She was already psyching herself out. This was as far as she'd ventured the previous day. She'd chickened out, limiting her experience to the view from the foyer. Today, she intended to inspect the entire downstairs with the hour she had available.

She took a big, shaky breath and relaxed her tense muscles.

You're good. This place has been dormant for twenty years. Just take it one room at a time.

She stepped farther into the shadows. To the right, through an archway she still saw in her dreams, the sitting room presented itself.

"Jesus."

Evidence of the fire spread across the scene like a cancer. Charred wood floorboards butted up against the soiled fireplace mantle, smoke-stained brick and plaster stretching all the way to the ceiling. A dark gray cloud seemed to hang in the room, but she realized it was smoke damage on the upper half of the walls. The areas where the couch, tables, and chairs once resided now sat empty, the lighter bare floors and walls in stark contrast to the burned streak blackening the center of the room.

A hellishly dark scar on the floor the size of her sister stared back at her from the center of it all.

"Oh, Constance." An unexpected, overwhelming surge of sadness climbed through her and constricted her throat. Tears seeped into her eyes, blurring her vision. Squeezing her eyes tight, she covered her face with her hands and lost sight of the room. Now blind, she spun on her heels to leave. Constance was right; she shouldn't be there. She was ignorant to think she'd stroll around the house undisturbed.

"Abigail?"

She froze, the soft, hopeful voice behind her lingering in her ears.

"Baby ..."

The warmth fled her body and the house grew utterly silent. Lowering her shaking hands and opening her eyes, she stood statuesque with her back to the house behind her. She tried to turn around, but her feet flailed, limp and ungrounded.

Confused, she looked down and saw her shadow below her on the dusty hardwood floor. Her confusion shifting to panic, she looked up at the dark front door. Slowly, the back of the door illuminated with reflected light as her body went rigid and rotated in the air. She moved like a puppet at the hands of a gentle puppeteer, her strings pulled taut, but not aggressively so. She had no control over her body.

As she turned in midair, the sitting room came into view. However, this time, the room appeared immaculately restored, just as it was in her youth. Someone had wiped all traces of that life-altering night back in 1966. The couch she'd cowered against, screaming and pinned beneath her dead mother's ghost, the coffee table, the adjacent sitting chairs and end tables ... everything in its right place.

She whipped into a panic, stray strands of her hair blowing in the breath blasting in and out of her nostrils. She tried to open her mouth but couldn't. Her teeth clenched tight against her will. At the last second, overwhelmed by fear, she closed her eyes, terrified of what she'd see as her body rotated toward the back of the house.

As if pulled by an invisible hand, she floated forward. She closed her eyes tight to avoid seeing the terrifying reality waiting for her. In her mind, she passed the sitting room entrance–*please don't pull me upstairs*–past the stairs, and toward the kitchenette. Bright light bloomed on the other side of her shut lids.

"Open your eyes, Abigail."

She squeezed her eyes tighter, fighting against the house. A breeze caressed her face and her eyes pried open despite her resistance. A desperate groan fled her throat as she winced against the blinding sunlight flooding through the kitchen window a few feet away.

Standing at the kitchen sink, her hands folded over her heart, was the most beautiful woman she'd ever seen. Her heart collapsed under the weight of uninterrupted love.

"Mama."

CHAPTER 9

CONSTANCE

Constance's vision blurred as she stared at the flashing green cursor on the computer screen. The morning's sentences were choppy and unnatural. She'd lost her voice and struggled with how poorly her thoughts translated to words.

"I need some fresh air." She pushed her chair away from the desk and stood, stretching her arms above her in awkward angles as she yawned. The flashing cursor danced in her vision everywhere she looked. She needed more caffeine. Blinking, she stepped around the edge of the desk and pulled the coffeepot from its base. The dark, steaming flow swirled in her cup as it poured. After topping her cup off with a dash of creamer, she abandoned the office for the short hallway.

"Shit." Constance reached back into the office and grabbed her coat from the hook on the back of the door. Shifting her coffee between hands, she shrugged into each arm of the coat as she walked down the gradually darkening hall to the backdoor. Leaning into the door, she pressed her way into the bright morning, careful not to tip her cup. The cold winter air pricked her exposed skin and seeped into the pores of her jeans as she propped the door open behind her. She reached into her left coat pocket and wrapped her fingers around the soft pack of Camels and a lighter. If Abigail found out she was smoking again, she'd kill her.

She set her coffee on the electrical meter, tipped the pack, and gently tapped a fresh cigarette out. Pushing the pack into her coat pocket, she lifted the cigarette to her lips, cupped her hands to block the breeze, and struck the lighter.

A flame exploded from the lighter, stealing her vision.

Constance dropped the lighter and recoiled defensively, the cigarette tumbling from her lips to her feet. Had the lighter exploded in her hand? She rubbed and blinked her eyes. As the world came into focus, the Whispering House filled the narrow lot behind the store.

She gasped and fell backward, sliding down the rough brick wall to the frigid pavement.

"No!" The house swelled as her voice echoed back at her from its neglected wood siding. Constance reached for the store's backdoor and found it shut and locked. She must have hit it when she fell against the building.

The keys. Get away.

Staring over her shoulder, eyes never leaving the house, she pulled herself up from the pavement and fished the keys from her pocket. Terror unraveled in her gut. How was this possible?

It's only a daydream.

The keys tumbled from her fingers to the pavement. She looked away from the house for a split second.

"Constance!" Abigail screamed from the house.

Constance's head shot up. She froze with her hand hovering just above the keys.

"Abigail!" she cried.

The house has her. Run.

Whimpering in fear, Constance sprinted from the safety of the building toward her nightmare.

"Abi! Where are you?"

"Constance!"

Every window on the house shot open, a symphony of screaming women's voices pouring forth. Constance flinched, then ran harder. Taking the front steps in two leaps, she crashed into the front door. She fumbled for the doorknob and shrieked when the blistering heat of the metal seared her palm. She pulled back reflexively. Then, against her control, her hand shot out and grabbed the glowing hot doorknob again.

Constance fell to her knees in agony, her hand sizzling and popping as her supple palm and fingers melted into the doorknob.

An invisible force coiled around her hand and up her arm, pulling her into the door as the windows on the porch exploded. The door burst into flames inches from her face.

One flaming hand emerged from the closed door above her shaking head, grabbed her by the coat and yanked her into the flames. A deafening, booming voice erased her thoughts as she crossed through the door and into another world.

HOOOOOOOOME

Constance screamed as her mind unraveled into burning streamers of grief and boundless fear. In the flames, she heard her mother's voice.

"Not like this. Please. Not like this."

No flames, total darkness.

Constance scrambled to her hands and knees in the dark, her panicked voice echoing off the hard surfaces of the silent, dormant house. She came to her feet and stole quick glimpses of her hands as her eyes darted around the house. She hadn't been there since the fire.

"This is just a dream. None of this is real," her words fell between hitching breaths. Her runaway pulse pounded in her neck, chest, and hands when she rubbed them. Sweat poured from her forehead into her eyes and soaked through her shirt and pants. Her body temp soared like she'd been on fire.

"It was just a dream," her mother's voice spoke from behind her.

Constance spun around and saw she was standing at the kitchen entrance. Her breath leaked from her open mouth as her mind stumbled over what she saw.

Her mother sat at the kitchenette table, cradling her little sister. Abigail couldn't have been over eight years old. Summer sunlight streamed through the window over the kitchen sink, casting shadows across the room. Dust the size of large snowflakes swirled, suspended in the light. The kitchen faucet dripped into the old farmhouse sink like a metronome.

Young Abigail buried her face in her mother's bosom. "I thought I'd lost you forever."

"Oh, baby. You'll never lose me. We'll be together forever, you and me."

"But what about when you die?" Abigail asked, her voice twisting with that last painful possibility.

"Even then, we'll be together. I'll never leave you."

Constance's knees buckled as her vision tipped up and away.

Abigail's voice tumbled to her across the shimmering webs between their dreams.

"Can Constance come with us?"

"Of course."

"Promise?"

"I promise."

CHAPTER 10

ABIGAIL

"Connie? Hello?"

Abigail walked down the hall from the bookstore's main office toward the bathroom and back door. She suspected she'd find her sister sneaking a cigarette out back. Constance knew she didn't approve of her nasty little habit, but at least she didn't smoke all the time—only when something frustrated her in one of her stories. She claimed it helped clear her thoughts when she got hung up on a plot hole or a misbehaving character.

The bathroom door stood open with the light out.

She must be out back.

Abigail pushed the back door open.

"Busted. I knew I'd find you out here."

Constance stood a few feet away, facing the field behind the store. Abigail looked down and saw a pack of cigarettes, a lighter, and a broken cigarette scattered on the ground around Constance's feet. A full cup of coffee sat on the electrical meter mounted to the brick exterior.

"Hey, are you okay?"

Constance turned to face her. Her eyes were bloodshot from the tears drying on her flushed cheeks. Her bleeding hands hung limp at her sides.

"I fell."

Abigail pulled a fresh gauze from the first aid kit sitting open on the checkout counter. She wrapped Constance's right hand and fastened the gauze with two pieces of medical tape on the back of her hand. "Now, can you tell me again how you fell?"

"I told you. I went outside to smoke a cigarette and the next thing I knew, I was on my hands and knees on the pavement."

"Did you get lightheaded?

"No. I didn't get lightheaded or trip. One moment I was standing and the next, I wasn't."

Abigail couldn't hide her skepticism. She pressed her lips together as she searched her sister's face for undisclosed answers. Constance was holding something back. She could tell because she wouldn't make eye contact.

"Connie, it's me. You can tell me if something happened."

"Asking more times won't change my answers. Drop it."

"Fine." She gathered the excess gauze, tape, and scissors and placed them into the kit. Pressing the red tin lid closed, she looked through the front windows at the empty parking lot. "Well, nothing like a little triage before a day of bookselling."

"So, are you going to tell me about your meetings with the contractors or what?" Constance asked.

Abigail paused before answering. She'd prepared for this conversation, but this situation with Constance had thrown her off.

"Oh, it was fine. I found a guy who's willing to do as much as we'll let them."

"Great. In that case, let them do everything." Constance lifted her bandaged hand and inspected Abigail's work. "How many contractors did you visit?"

"Just the one," Abigail responded before realizing she'd just set a trap for herself. She turned, hoping Constance wouldn't get curious about how long she'd been gone if she'd only met with one contractor. "But they took forever."

"Really? It took you that long to talk to them?"

Abigail nodded. "You know how these county folk are. They aren't in any rush. I had to remind the guy several times that I had to run so I could open the store and he just kept talking like I hadn't said a word." She sensed Constance staring at her from the side.

"I don't believe you."

"Come on, let's not do this," Abigail pleaded.

Constance narrowed her eyes. "You went to the house. Didn't you?"

"No. I did not."

"Look me in the eye and say it."

Abigail lifted her face to meet Constance's harsh gaze. "What is your problem? Did you hit your head when you fell?"

"Don't do that. You're trying to change the subject. Say it."

"This is ridiculous. I'm not playing games with you this morning." Abigail walked to the end of the counter and organized a stack of business cards and bookmarks she must straighten every hour.

"You're lying to me again. I know it," Constance said.

"You call me a liar? You won't tell me what happened to you out back. You think I'm buying your story?"

"There isn't a story," Constance snapped back.

"Yeah? Well, then what do you call that crap you made up about falling out back? Oh, that's right. It's a *lie*."

Abigail's body temperature climbed. She hated being questioned. Ironically, she was upset with Constance for putting her in a position to lie to her. If she hadn't been so damn unreasonable, Abigail wouldn't have to sneak around behind her back.

"And why are you so convinced I went to the house, huh? Want to tell me that?"

"Because it doesn't make sense that you spent so long with one contractor."

"But why does it have to be the house? You didn't assume I stopped at the post office or Office Suppliers to grab a few things?"

"It doesn't take a genius to see that you didn't bring any mail or shopping bags in with you." Constance stood a little taller, raising her eyebrows as she landed her intelligent counterstrike.

Abigail quickly rebounded. "Maybe there wasn't any mail. My point is you assume I'm up to no good without evidence."

Now Constance looked uncomfortable. Her eyes dropped to her bandage for a moment and she drew a shaky breath. It was apparent this turn of the conversation unsettled her.

Abigail continued. "I come back from talking with the contractor and find you standing in a daze, with your hands bleeding and your stuff all over the ground. What's *your* deal? You didn't have another episode, did you?" Hearing the question out loud convinced her that Constance was hiding something troubling.

"You don't know what you're talking about. I'm done with this conversation. One of us has to be an adult here."

The bell chimed over the door as someone entered. Abigail turned and saw Mrs. Harting ease the door shut behind her. Abigail put on her best smile.

"Good morning, Mrs. Harting. Looking for a particular book today?"

"Good morning, dear. No, thank you. I'm just looking around."

"Of course. Let me know if I can help you with anything."

Abigail turned back to Constance, but she was gone. She must have retreated to the office to avoid interacting with Mrs. Harting.

The woman came in every few days and never bought a thing, which made sense since she'd been dead for five years.

CHAPTER II

ABIGAIL

The day flew by in that weird way only slow winter days can. Time dragged after lunch, but the sun rushed the night along as it fell into the westward trees, and the temperatures plummeted to freezing.

"Geez, where did the day go?" Abigail asked as she locked the store's front door and walked against the stiff, bitter breeze on their way to the Honda. Constance had said little since their argument that morning, and that was fine with Abigail. The less they interacted, the less opportunity there was to bring up the house.

Despite her reluctance to talk about her morning, Abigail was bursting at the seams with joy about her trip to the house. She looped the dreamlike exchange through her head the entire way home, turning her head when the impulse to smile struck her. She couldn't tell Constance about seeing Mama. Not yet, at least.

The girls retired for the night after a simple dinner of Campbell's chicken noodle soup and grilled cheese sandwiches. Abigail took a quick shower, threw on a set of flannel pajamas, and settled into the plush embrace of her oversized comforter. However, sleep did not come easily. Her experience at the house that morning refused to leave her thoughts. Laying in total darkness, her mind flipped through images of her mother standing before the kitchen sink, her upturned face brilliantly illuminated by the summer light streaming through the window. The memory worked her heart into a deep throb. They'd finally met again outside of her dreams.

Or had they?

Perhaps the whole thing was some sort of next-level daydream, the type of borderline hallucination she read about in her favorite psychological horror books. How else could she explain the conflict between what she knew and what she saw?

Her mother had died in 1966. Yet now, she inhabited the house. The home had been vacant and neglected for so many years. But the kitchen still looked just as it had in her youth.

And their physical relationship, severed by death all those painful years ago, now reconnected, rejoined without seams, beautiful and ethereal.

But had it happened, or was it some surreal daydream? Her doubts surfaced as the time stacked, each minute a small dose of reality obscuring her perception of their time in the kitchen that morning.

What if this was an unforeseen reaction to being in the house again? Could she have experienced some trauma-induced confusion?

Abigail glanced at the glowing red digits on the nightstand's alarm clock, realizing forty-five minutes had passed. But she was no closer to falling asleep than she was when she climbed into bed. Reading usually cleared her mind and brought her closer to sleep, so she grabbed her hardcover copy of *The Talisman* and a small book light from the nightstand. She'd read every book Stephen King had published to date, but this was her first taste of Peter Straub. So far, she loved what they'd fed her.

Shortly after, she slipped into a strange space between dreams and her new reality.

Abigail stood facing the woods behind the Whispering House. Despite the engorged moon hanging low and bright in the cloudless sky, the yard was an uninterrupted darkness, a black ocean spanning between her and the trees encroaching on the clearing. To her right, she barely saw the path to the family cemetery. A soft yellow glow interrupted the night behind her. She turned her head away from the woods and toward the light's origin. The window over the kitchen sink appeared like an orb floating on the face of the dark house. Abigail's heart stumbled as Delilah stepped into the window frame and lowered her head. Abigail realized her mother was crying.

"No Mama. Don't cry."

"She's been waiting for you." A voice broke over her shoulder. Abigail spun, her breath catching in her chest, and came face-to-face with her dead cousin, Adeline.

Flawless in the pale moonlight, the girl looked like art. Her round eyes glistened, bouncing starlight to the heavens. Two tight, perfect braids of hair cascaded down the front of each shoulder.

"Look," Adeline commanded, raising a hand.

A force like hands cradled Abigail's head and followed her cousin's hand. Slowly, the girl extended her arm and pointed one finger.

The shed.

The two shed doors slowly opened in unison. In the growing gap between them, a swarm of fireflies drifted out, illuminating the yard below. In their light, the ground undulated. Abigail gasped when she saw a million tiny black orbs reflecting firefly light.

Those orbs—those are eyes.

Starling eyes.

Abigail groaned as she realized she stood in a sea of silent starlings. Memories of the birds from her youth in synchronized flight above the house filled her mind. The birds covered the ground in all directions, pressing their mass to the woods, the house, and beyond. She tried to turn her head toward Adeline, to plead with her to stop, but she couldn't budge. She was fully under Adeline's control.

"Don't … hurt … me."

Adeline spoke from the periphery of her vision. "Do what's right. Help them."

The cloud of fireflies pouring from the open shed intensified.

None of this was possible. Where were they coming from? How were there so many of them?

It's just a dream. I need to wake up.

Adeline snapped her fingers, abruptly arresting Abigail's will to fight. "Help them."

"I can't. I don't want to lose her." Overwhelmed by grief, the sobs came in a flood. Her chest and shoulders shuttered with each labored breath. She knew what Adeline wanted, but she couldn't follow her orders. It would break her.

"Please, Adeline. I'm begging. Don't make me do this."

"Help them."

The ground stirred as the birds craned their heads toward the girls standing rigid in the center of the yard.

"You must tell her the truth. It's the only way to set things right."

"Never," Abigail whispered defiantly.

Adeline's pointing hand dropped to her side and the ground erupted in a battery of starlings. Abigail's body briefly returned to her before the birds overtook them, blacking out the moon and drowning Abigail's cries.

Abigail sat on the edge of her bed in the tiny room. She'd woken from the dream whimpering and panting. Her heart beat hard in her chest, her mind spinning with trace images of the starlings staring up at her from the yard, a sea of eyes probing her soul.

"Oh, Adeline. I didn't expect to see you tonight," she said in a low voice. Many years had passed since she'd last dreamed of her dead cousin.

It's the house, you know. It's talking to you.

"No. It's just a dream." She shifted her weight to her weary feet and stood, unsure where they intended to take her. She looked at the alarm clock's sharp red digits.

3:13

She groaned at the thought of how little sleep she'd had. This would sting later when the early afternoon sun warmed the bookstore, and the emptiness laid its stifling silence on her like a weighted blanket.

Passing through the wood-trimmed bedroom doorway, she entered the dark, narrow hall stretching between her room and the rest of the home. A light over the kitchen sink at the opposite end of the house cast an eerie glow and deepened the shadows of the surrounding corridor. She rubbed the sleep from her eyes as she went, navigating the hall on autopilot. The floorboards clicked and popped beneath her weight as she neared Constance's partially open bedroom door. Abigail leaned close to peer through the gap at her sister when a noise in the hall started her. Her breath caught in her chest when the bathroom door opened to her right and a harsh light bit her eyes.

Constance strolled in a daze from the open bathroom. Her face looked like a sagging mask. She caught sight of Abigail and her left hand shot to her breast in surprise.

"Jesus, Abigail. What are you doing up? You nearly gave me a heart attack." Her right hand lingered on the light switch behind her, her eyes squinting.

"Leave it on, I'm next. A dream woke me and I couldn't fall back asleep, so here we are. Hall party at three in the morning."

"What kind of dream?" Constance asked.

Abigail skirted past her sister and slid through the partially open bathroom door. Her eyes throbbed against the lights bordering the bathroom mirror. The toilet sat nestled between the small vanity cabinet and the shower on the left wall. She left the door cracked behind her, pushed her pants down, and sat on the toilet.

"Earth to Abi. What kind of dream?" Constance asked again.

"I don't remember," Abigail lied.

"How can you not remember? It was enough to wake you."

Abigail closed her eyes and released her bladder. The sound of her urine hitting the water broke the silence and gave her an excuse to stall her response to Constance's question. She took a different approach.

"You're up. Did you have a dream too?"

Now Constance stalled on the other side of the cracked door.

"Yes."

Abigail finished, wiped, stood, and tied her pajama pants as she approached the small sink to wash her hands. Constance eased the door open a few inches, her eyes cast down to avoid the direct light. Her scarred face presented itself in devastating detail in the open doorway like a mask adorned with a mildly skewed, narrow nose, webbed eyelids, pocked and ridged cheeks, and lips aligned but of abnormal thickness.

Abigail's heart sank as she lathered her soapy hands together in the freezing tap water. "We've got a lot on our minds, that's all."

"No. I don't think that's it," Constance said. She hesitated, then continued. "It's the house. I saw it in my dream tonight."

The tile floor turned frigid beneath Abigail's bare feet and her stomach rolled. Constance's revelation kicked her mind into another gear.

"What happened? Were you in the house?" Images of the burned sitting room from her visit rushed back to Abigail.

That massive charred scar on the floor. That's hers. Constance owns all the scars.

"I wasn't in the house. I was in the backyard."

Abigail dried her hands on the towel hanging to her left and faced Constance, who didn't appear interested in letting her leave the bathroom yet.

"It was night and there were millions of those dark birds covering the entire yard. They opened a path to the cemetery, but I was too afraid to go. I couldn't."

"You don't have to, Connie. You never have to go back there again."

"I saw her. I saw Mama standing in the kitchen window."

Needles pressed into her hands and feet as the blood rushed from her extremities to her core. Her heart raced. "I don't feel good."

"Let's get you back to bed," Constance said.

"Okay." Abigail flipped the light off and floated down the dark hall to her room with Constance in tow. How had they had such similar dreams? The yard, the starlings, the cemetery path.

She hadn't mentioned the shed.

Thank God.

But Constance *had* mentioned their mother for the first time since they'd inherited the house. That was not alright.

Abigail crossed her room in a nauseous stumble and climbed onto her bed. Constance stayed at the door.

"Can I do anything for you? Need some water?"

"No, thank you. We just need some sleep."

"Okay." Constance lingered. "I love you."

"I love you too." Abigail closed her eyes and spent the rest of the early morning suspended just above sleep and just below awareness.

CHAPTER 12

ABIGAIL

Exhaustion overtook Abigail as she huddled over a cup of piping hot coffee at the small kitchen table. Her mind mushed, spread, and reconstructed snippets of the night's dreams and waking moments as she watched fine specs of coffee bean swirl on the surface of her drink. Constance remained in her room, either sleeping or lounging in complete silence.

Abigail's heart beat slowly in her heavy chest. Her lack of sleep over the past few nights, the stress of the house, and life in the melancholy winter of this quiet little county all weighed on her. The world seemed hellbent on unraveling while somehow remaining frozen. The house had brought her back to her mother in a dreamlike assault, yet she carried out her perilously monotonous life.

The kitchen phone rang on the wall beside Abigail's head, its shrill mechanical bell breaking her daze. Her right hand shot to the phone. Bringing the receiver to her head a little too fast, the hard plastic smacked her skull just above her ear. She exhaled in frustration as she answered. "Ugh, hello?"

"Well, good morning to you, too. It's Eli."

"Hey. Thank God it's you. I couldn't handle a telemarketer this early."

Eli laughed. "Sorry for cutting straight to the point but, I have a client meeting in a minute. Are you available to meet me at the house at nine this morning? I want to get a good look at the interior and my schedule's slammed the rest of the week, so this may be my only opportunity."

Abigail processed his request against the schedule in her mind. "Yeah, that works. I can be there earlier if you'd like."

"I can't make it there any earlier, but I'll be there at nine sharp for sure. Okay, gotta run. See ya soon."

Eli ended the call, and Abigail returned the receiver to the wall mount. She glanced at the clock mounted above the kitchen counter. The minute and hour hands pointed to a quarter past seven. She had plenty of time to swing by the store and process some inventory before meeting Eli. Or she could go to the house early …

I could see Mama again.

Anticipation crept into her gut as she realized she may experience the house differently with someone else there. Would she see her mother with Eli present? If she did, would he see her, too?

"He'd be terrified," she said aloud.

Doubt crept in. Her visions were *hers*. The house—their mother—wanted to see her girls. She'd have no use for Eli.

She had to go early.

"Who was that?"

Constance's voice startled her. Abigail flinched, her hand striking her cup. A small wave of coffee breached the cup's lip and ran down its side to the table.

"Shit," Abigail hissed.

"Calm down, it's just me. Sit. I'll get you a paper towel." Constance crossed the kitchen and grabbed a paper towel from the stand beside the sink.

"You startled me. I didn't know you were creeping around."

"I see that. Next time, jump a little higher, okay?" Constance brought the paper towel to her. "I was asleep until the phone rang. Don't take offense, but I'm not going to the store today. I'm staying here to catch up on some research for the book."

"Sounds good." Abigail wiped the spilled coffee from her cup and tabletop.

"So, who called?"

"Oh, that was the contractor. They want to meet me at the house, so I'm going to head out." Abigail looked up into Constance's puffy, down-turned face. She searched her sister's damaged features for signs of disapproval and found none.

"They'll be there with you?" Constance asked.

Abigail hesitated, then nodded. "Yep. We'll get their task list started so they can get to work, and we can put the house on the market and move on with our lives." Abigail smiled to arrest any hesitation Constance may be hiding.

"Well, call me when you get to the store, so I know you're okay. As much as I like the idea of you being with someone, it also makes me nervous for you to be alone with a stranger."

"You're sweet. I'll be fine. This guy is harmless." She moved to another topic before Constance challenged her assumption. "It should be a quiet day in the store. I have some new thrillers to unpack, but that's about it."

"Cool." Constance yawned. She opened the refrigerator door, withdrew the creamer, then returned to the counter and poured a cup of coffee. Abigail watched her as she went, momentarily mesmerized by Constance's fluid movement. Familiarity brought a haunting déjà vu to Abigail. In her mind, she saw their mother moving across the kitchen in her youth. The ache in Abigail's chest blossomed again.

Mama.

Abigail's pulse raced, her hand hovering inches from the doorknob.

"Don't be a baby. Just open the door."

The freezing morning air soaked into her clothes as she stalled on the porch. She didn't trust the uncertainty waiting on the other side of the door. Would she find her mother waiting in beautiful streaming sunlight again?

What if she found nothing but an empty house? What if her last experience with her mother was truly her last?

Finding nothing may be a worse fate than finding danger. She needed—no, *craved*—her mother. Her anticipation made her jumpy and unsettled. She needed answers.

Abigail closed her eyes, grabbed the knob, and changed her life forever.

Abigail surfaced in overwhelming bliss.

Utter and complete euphoria submerged in sour grief forced conflicted tears from her eyes and obscured her vision.

"Don't cry, baby."

Abigail's breath moved in and out of her mouth in sweet, barely perceptible puffs, kissing her lips in each passage.

Her body seemed foreign and small. She squeezed her eyes to release a fresh flow of tears, then looked down at her tiny hands folded in her lap. Delilah cradled her on the sitting room couch.

I'm a child.

The realization terrified her. She looked up, seeking answers in her mother's face. Delilah's brilliant blue eyes met hers and matched the vaporous light swirling around them like mist. Chocolate curls framed her smooth face and cascaded down her shoulders. Her lips looked full, rose tinged and moist.

She was *alive*.

"What's happening?" Abigail barely heard her own voice over soothing dissonant tones ringing in her ears like an ensemble of violins.

"We're together, baby. This is eternal love."

"It hurts, Mama,"

Abigail's heart collapsed another notch. How could she ever come back from this?

"Oh, Abi. No more tears. We never have to be apart again."

"Am I ... am I still alive? Why am I little?"

Delilah laughed. "Of course you're alive. What a silly question to ask."

"Well, you're—"

"I'm here."

"But you aren't supposed to be. I lost you."

Abigail looked toward the floor in the center of the room and barely saw the cancerous, charred floorboard through the swirling light. Delilah's fingers met her chin and turned her face back to her.

"Mama, we lost you. You know that, right?"

Delilah's smile faltered for a second, her eyes blinking while locked on Abigail's like an android experiencing a forced reboot. Her eyes regained their clarity.

"I'm here. As long as you're here, I'm here."

Abigail squirmed, but couldn't move her legs. Her mother continued.

"Me, you, and your sister. This is our home. We can stay here together as long as we'd like."

"But, aren't you supposed to ..." Abigail considered her words, "... move on?"

"I don't understand." Delilah's brows bunched together. Abigail saw emotion brewing behind her mother's rigid demeanor.

"You know. Like to heaven?"

Delilah's pupils dilated to pinpoints. A single tear fled her right eye to join her smile. Her lips quaked. "I don't understand," she repeated.

"Mama, you're dead."

"Love never dies, Abi." The quaking intensified. "Now stop worrying about such lofty things. A girl your age ..." Delilah's words trailed off as her gaze drifted toward the front windows.

Abigail followed her eyes. The haze surrounding them slowly thinned, revealing a long, dark object on the other side of the room. Sunlight penetrated the front windows, further complicating their visibility.

Delilah's casket emerged from the haze.

Terrified, Abigail looked up at her mother. Delilah's face had lost its light. Her eyes were cold, hard, and distant. Delilah's mouth slowly opened and spoke, soft and dreamlike.

"The sun is setting. Go outside and call for your sister."

"Mama. Look at me."

"Do what I asked."

"Mama, Constance can't come here. You don't understand."

Delilah looked down at her daughter. Her eyes harbored something dark and desperate. "Help me, Abi."

Abigail watched in terror as her mother became transparent. Abigail's body slowly lowered to the couch.

"Mama!" She reached for her mother's face, but her hands passed through her as she fully dissipated.

DRIP DRIP DRIP

Abigail snapped her eyes to the ceiling. Black water ran in a line from one end of the ceiling to the other, dripping to the burned floorboards.

The casket lurched on its stand in front of the darkening windows. Someone beat on the lid from inside.

Abigail scrambled across the couch, drawing her legs to her chest.

Don't panic. Don't panic.

Black water breached the gaps in the casket lid. It lurched again as its captive raged within.

"No. No!"

Abigail ran for the archway and into the foyer. She gained speed and skirted past the casket, fearing her mother—or someone else—would force the lid open and unravel whatever sanity remained in her confusion.

She yanked the front door open and reemerged in winter as a grown woman. The door slammed hard behind her as she stumbled down the porch steps and ran for her car.

Once in the car, keys rattling in her shaking fingers, Abigail broke down. A conflicted mix of emotion surged in her—love, guilt, excitement, outright terror. Fear kept her moving despite the tears blurring her vision.

She backed out of the driveway without looking behind her, then barreled away from the house toward town.

A mile down the road, she passed Eli's truck in the opposite lane. They exchanged a momentary glance as the vehicles whipped past each other. Then she saw his brake lights illuminate in her rearview mirror.

Abigail kept driving. She had no intention of turning around and meeting Eli at the house. Plans had changed. She didn't know what she'd do about the house, but she knew repairing and selling it was no longer possible.

Pressing her foot to the gas pedal, she muttered, "I won't lose you again."

CHAPTER 13

CONSTANCE

The coziness of the small family room couch threatened to lull Constance back to sleep. Although she'd already been awake an hour and had finished her first cup of coffee, she fought to keep her eyes open as she read. Dickens simply wasn't a safe read when she was tired.

Constance pulled the throw blanket tighter around her chest and wiggled lower onto the couch. To her right, a large picture window revealed a cinematic view of their quiet street. A visible layer of frost coated the frigid winter day. Their rancher sat on the outer loop of a sleepy neighborhood and from her vantage point in the family room, she could see the frozen quarter acre front yard and the two houses facing them across the street. Rather uneventful brick ranchers with single car garages and bordering trees, the houses represented typical Virginia middle-class dwellings. Constance was perfectly content staying there for the rest of her life. It became her home when they joined Aunt Jenny and Uncle Hank there twenty years prior. Twenty years of silent, peaceful existence. Now, without Aunt Jenny in the house, it was just her and Abigail.

Eyes drifting over the open book in her lap, her mind roamed far from the words on the pages as they blurred, reformed, and blurred again.

Darkness, then light. She dozed in and out of the morning.

Darkness.

Light.

Darkness.

The world gradually constricted around Constance.

Tighter. Tighter still.

Muffled voices. Familiar but years away. One young, one older, but not elder.

The scent of minerals eased into her nostrils. Water? But she didn't feel rain on her skin. She felt nothing but the couch cushions cuddled to her right arm.

The blanket slid from her legs and exposed her bare feet in the absolute darkness. She wiggled her toes but felt nothing.

She shifted her weight on the cushions, but again felt nothing.

Did I fall asleep? *That would explain the lack of feeling.*

A dim, golden light glowed to her right. She tried to move, but her head remained fixed forward. Numb and unable to budge, she panicked.

A wall of white silk baffling appeared, reflecting the source of gold light growing at her side.

Her mind cleared, and her vision followed. She looked at her immobile feet. A black dress covered her body down to her ankles.

Darkness. The smell of water. Black dress in gold light.

A horrid memory surfaced ugly and harsh. Visions of being trapped in the casket with Adel—

"Welcome home, Constance."

An unseen force rotated her head to the right and Adeline came into focus, the dark bird affixed underarm like a doll. Adeline's eyes glowed gold like dimming headlights on an old car. She looked exactly as she had in Constance's youth.

"I'm dreaming. This isn't really happening," Constance pleaded aloud.

The muffled voices swelled outside, so familiar…

"They're here," Adeline said flatly and without emotion.

"Abi?"

Adeline spoke, "Yes."

Constance tried to move, but her body refused. She ordered her hands to hammer, her feet to kick, but nothing happened. She lay paralyzed.

"Not paralyzed," Adeline said.

"Why can't I move? Why is this happening?"

The starling's head rotated toward Constance, matching the angle of Adeline's face.

"It's time. If she'll allow it," Adeline said. Her mouth moved inches from Constance's face, but she couldn't feel the girl's breath on her skin. She remained numb.

Constance's mind unfolded and expanded. The world grew bigger despite the confines of the tight casket. An inevitable force pulled her closer.

"Soon, Constance."

Water came into view, slowly rising around them in the claustrophobic box. The black liquid obscured the vision of her right eye first.

"No, Adeline. Please!"

"Soon."

Head frozen in place, black water poured into her mouth, climbed her lips and violated her nose, then stole her vision.

Constance screamed into the black depths as her hands and feet broke free from their bonds and met the sealed coffin lid above.

CHAPTER 14

ABIGAIL

Abigail parked her car at a careless angle behind the bookstore and left it running. This would only take a minute.

Unlocking the rear door, she entered the bookstore. She hurried down the short hall past the bathroom on her left and the office on her right and emerged behind the counter in the storefront. She shuffled a few binders under the counter and withdrew a green folder. Flipping it open and spilling several loose pieces of printer paper to the countertop, Abigail withdrew a folded sheet of legal sized paper. She grabbed a fat-tipped blue marker from a small white basket of pens under the cash register and scrawled a makeshift sign.

CLOSED FOR A FAMILY EVENT
THANK YOU FOR YOUR PATIENCE

Abigail gathered the loose papers into the folder and tossed it under the counter. Trading the marker for a roll of scotch tape, she taped the sign to the glass door, where arriving patrons would clearly see it above the handle.

Abigail deposited the tape on the counter, left the storefront, traversed the hall, and breached the back door. She pressed the door shut until the latch engaged and locked behind her.

Back in the Honda, she took a series of deep breaths and turned up the heat before pulling away from the building and heading for Eli's office.

"Honestly, I'm not upset." Eli stood behind his desk with a closed notepad in one hand. "I can't imagine how difficult it must be visiting that place after everything you went through."

Abigail stood in his office doorway, nervously winding her fingers into one other. "Thank you. But I still feel terrible. You're super busy and you made the trip out there for nothing. I'm sorry I wimped out."

Eli walked around his desk and crossed the large office, stopping a few feet from her.

"I guess I'm just not ready to do anything with the house yet," Abigail said. "I'll take some time to think things through and when the time's right, I'll call you."

"That's fine. But hear me out for a minute. You may not like this proposal, but we can do this without you. You could give me a key to the house, and I'd take care of everything and let you know when we're done."

"No way. I would never ask you to take this entire project on by yourself," she said.

Eli laughed, "Trust me, I wouldn't be the one doing all the work. My crew would take care of the labor. I'd just make sure it all got done. The point is, you wouldn't have to be there."

"I appreciate that. Let me think about it."

"Sure." He stepped closer, now only two feet separating them in the doorway. "Look, we both know the work needs to get done, whether you sell the house or keep it. Now or later, it doesn't really matter. I'm not convinced you should be involved either way. I'm your friend, and I hate to see you this upset. You've been a mess since you flew in here this morning."

Abigail hid from this truth by diverting her eyes to her shoes. "Thanks, Eli. You sure know how to make a girl feel pretty." She forced an exaggerated smile to lighten the mood.

"You know what I mean," he said with a playful sigh. "I mean it. You're like a sister to me. I know you better than most people do, and I can tell this morning beat you up. When the time is right, swing in, drop the keys off, and we'll get started. Deal?"

"Deal," Abigail conceded. She had no intentions of honoring his request, but she needed this conversation to end. There was nothing more to discuss today.

"Cool. Now, scram. I've got a meeting to attend, and you have books to sell. For the love of God, this town needs all the culture it can get."

"Thanks, Eli." She pulled him into a tight hug, drawing comfort from the brief physical contact. It was the first time she'd embraced a man in years. "I'll see ya soon. Thanks again."

"You've got it. Now, act like a tree and—"

"Watch it, pal," she jokingly pushed him and left his office. She nearly walked right into two towering men wearing flannel shirts, stonewashed jeans, and too much aftershave.

"Good morning," the guy on the right said. She didn't make eye contact or look at him long enough to determine whether they knew each other. Instead, she nodded and kept her head down, sliding past them as quickly as possible. She was in no mood for small talk, and she had somewhere to be.

As Abigail walked past the front counter, Dee spotted her and tried to start a conversation.

"Oh, Abigail! I didn't even see you come in this morning! How's life?"

Damn it.

"Sorry, Dee. No time to talk today. Gotta run." Abigail exited through the front door without missing a step. She had one last place to visit before heading home to level with her sister.

"Girl, get in here and out of the cold. You're likely to freeze your britches off out there." Glenda propped the door open with one arm while Abigail hustled up the paved walkway to the real estate office. "Lord help us. I can't wait for spring to get here. Go on into my office. The heater's kicking in there."

Abigail shuttled through the waiting room and into the office and unbuttoned her coat as she took a seat. "I feel like I was just here yesterday," she said, making small talk to ease herself into the uncomfortable conversation ahead.

Glenda took her coat from her and set it on a rack standing beside the door.

"What brings you in this morning, dear? You aren't getting cold feet about the house, are you?"

Damn!

Abigail wondered if her expression had revealed her concerns or if Glenda had received a tip from Dee over the phone while she was driving. That sounded likely considering small town gossip and all.

"Not necessarily, but I need to delay putting it on the market. I hope it isn't too much of an inconvenience."

"Give me that coat. Let's get you something to drink. Then you can tell me all about your plans. Hot tea?"

"Sure. Hot tea sounds great."

Glenda hollered toward the lobby through the open door. "Can you bring us two cups of hot tea, Chrissy?"

"Yes, ma'am."

"Great." Glenda took her seat across from Abigail and grabbed a round, Christmas themed tin container from the coffee table between them. "Would you like some fudge? My sister brought me a ton for Christmas and I'm doing my best to give it away."

"Oh. I really shouldn't."

"Smart girl," Glenda said, dropping the tin container to the table. "That stuff will stick with you." She looked behind Abigail at the doorway. "Oh good, here's the tea. Thank you, Chrissy."

Abigail turned in her chair and took the cup as Chrissy handed it to her. "Thank you so much." Steam danced above her cup and the scent of bergamot and honey wafted into the air.

"I could drink this stuff all day," Glenda said. "Okay, so what's on our mind, Ms. Abigail?"

Abigail took a deep breath. "I suppose I just wanted to update you on my progress with things. I've hired Tri-County to handle the repairs and get the house ready for the market."

"Oh, they're outstanding. Eli does great work."

"Yes, he does. And as you know, we're very close friends, so he was my first choice and thankfully, he agreed to take the project." Abigail sipped her tea. "So, he'll get rolling soon. I tried to accompany him on a walkthrough of the home this morning and I chickened out. I thought I'd be okay in the house, but I was wrong." She looked away, embarrassed to hear herself admit out loud how the house affected her. Of course, Eli and Glenda's understanding of her experience with the home differed considerably from the truth.

"Oh, honey. Give yourself some grace. You've been through a lot lately. We don't have to talk about this now if it's not a good time."

"No, I'm fine." Abigail straightened in her chair, regretting dropping her guard for a moment. "We're good."

"Okay. And you're hiring Eli and his gang to do the work so you don't have to be there, right?"

"Yes. They're onboard and I'm very grateful."

"Good. When will they start work?"

Abigail met Glenda's eyes. "In a few weeks."

"Oh. That long?"

"Yes. They're booked up and will get to us in a few weeks. In the meantime, this will give me time to get things in order for the sale. So, good news, we're not in a rush."

"I see." It was Glenda's turn to inspect her tea. "Are we talking three to four weeks or ten to twelve?"

"I suppose somewhere in the middle. The soonest he'll get started is four weeks from now."

"Right. Well, I think you'll hit the market at a great time. Things are slow around here until it warms up, anyway." Glenda laughed, but she sounded disappointed.

"I'm terribly sorry for the inconvenience. I know you were ready to get this thing moving. But I suppose this is God's way of telling us it's not the right time yet."

Glenda settled back into her chair and smiled. "I suppose so. Look, I know this is a lot and I know you aren't excited about selling. But in the end, I think you'll be relieved when that house is finally off your hands and the money is in your bank account. Amen?" Glenda raised her tea.

"Amen," Abigail raised hers as well. She sipped to conclude the toast, then continued. "Honestly, I wish I could stay there forever. There's something special about that place."

Glenda's smile remained in place but lost its energy. She rested her cup on her right thigh and took a deep breath. "I can see why you'd see it that way. But I don't see you staying there. Not when you've inherited your aunt's place and stand to make some solid coin on the farmhouse. I mean, how can you turn that down?"

"Well, there's more to life than money. That's for damn sure," Abigail said.

"Right, but money sure makes those things in life easier, am I right? Besides—and I don't mean to upset you by saying this—that place is a constant reminder of some pretty dark times for your family. Letting that place go could do wonders for your sanity."

"What's that supposed to mean?" Abigail asked, irritation creeping into her tone.

"I'm sorry. I didn't mean to sound crass. It's just that you've been through so much there and that leaves marks on a person. You know?"

"Yeah. I know. But it also strengthens you. I may have lost quite a bit because of that house, but I also stand to gain quite a bit. Sanity intact or not." She flashed a toothy grin and downed the last of her hot tea. The concluding swig of tea always held the strongest flavor.

"Good."

Abigail stood, signaling the end of the meeting and her intent to leave. Glenda followed her lead.

"Well, I really should get going. Thanks for giving me a few minutes of your morning."

"Of course," Glenda replied. "Just keep me posted, okay?"

"You've got my word." Abigail set her cup on the coffee table and gathered her coat from the rack beside the door. As she left the office and the comforting scent of tea behind, she realized the sun was approaching its zenith in the late morning sky.

She gave Glenda a last wave as she climbed into her car and decided she was finally ready to go home.

CHAPTER 15

ABIGAIL

Abigail entered the house with an unusually aggressive shove of the door. The doorknob slipped from her grip and the door collided with the adjacent wall.

"Damn."

She needed to slow down. Anticipating a complicated discussion with Constance had her nerves in a knot. She looked around the empty family room.

"Connie, where are you hiding? Hello?"

Perhaps she was resting in her room or using the bathroom. Abigail peeked into the empty kitchen before walking down the narrow hall toward Constance's room. She passed the empty bathroom on the left and saw Constance's bedroom door open across the hall. She stopped at her sister's closed door and listened for two silent seconds before knocking lightly.

No answer.

She turned the knob and eased the door open. The room looked sterile and completely undisturbed, just as it always did. The perfectly made bed centered the room, and every book, figurine, and desktop knickknack sat exactly where they'd been for as long as she could remember. Abigail's blood ran cold. Something was terribly wrong.

She felt it in her bones.

Something fell in the family room.

She was probably out back, and just came inside.

No, that didn't seem right. The sound came from the family room, not the back door. Abigail cast her eyes down the hall as she slowly backed out of the bedroom into the hall. She stopped and listened.

Nothing.

Abigail rotated in place and took one step toward the front of the house when another item fell in the family room.

Abigail's pulse pounded in her temples. A thin layer of sweat emerged across her body.

"Connie?" She picked up her pace but stepped lightly. Again, she passed the empty bathroom and reached the point where the hall met the family room and foyer. She didn't see anyone or anything amiss. Not yet, at least.

She stole a quick glance through the kitchen doorway on her left and returned her attention to the family room. The television set was off, the door remained shut, and the curtains hanging on both sides of the picture window swayed in an imperceptible breeze. She stepped farther into the room and noticed Constance's blanket spread across the couch cushions.

Abigail's body went rigid.

An open book lay on the floor beside the couch.

A starling stood on its open pages, staring directly at Abigail without moving.

CHIRP CHIRP CHIRP

Every nerve in Abigail's body came alive.

How did that thing get in here?

The starling chirped again and danced in place on the open book.

The world spun, and Abigail doubled over in pain. Without warning, a solid column of black water shot up through her throat and out through her mouth. She dropped to her knees as her stomach cramped into a ball and tears filled her eyes. She arched her back and gasped for air before the next torrent of liquid filled her throat and blew from her nose and mouth with incredible pressure.

Images of black water pouring from the closed lid of her mother's casket earlier that morning blitzed her memory.

On the floor beside the couch, the starling danced on the open book. Abigail tried to scoot back and away from the bird, her fingers slipping on the saturated beige carpet.

The starling's wings beat the pages and Abigail flew backward as if a hurricane had blown through the picture window.

She crashed into the wall bordering the kitchen and almost lost consciousness. Scrambling to her feet, the geyser of black liquid subsided. Her soaked clothes clung to her body like webs.

Run!

Coughing and gasping for air, Abigail stumbled to the foyer. She yanked the large wooden door open and fell across the short porch and down the front steps to the yard. Frigid winter air penetrated her wet clothes and drove spikes of clarity into her mind. She crawled to her car and pulled herself up on the bumper. The front door of the house slowly swung shut. She squeezed her eyes and coughed the remaining liquid from her lungs. Now able to think again, her mind clamored for answers.

The starling. The black water. Constance disappearing.

The house.

"She can't be." Abigail struggled to believe what her intuition demanded.

There's no way Constance would go to that house.

"She's there."

Abigail spun around and nearly screamed at the sight of Mrs. Harting's ghost standing in the yard.

"She's there."

This was the first time Abigail had seen the woman's ghost outside the bookstore. Her mind skipped like a fouled record when she tried to speak.

"How do you—you—"

"She needs you, Abigail. Go, *now*."

The urgency of her command moved Abigail to action. Leaning on the car for support, she slid along the front fender to the driver's side door and climbed into the Honda. She started the engine, threw the transmission in reverse, and bottomed out when the car bounced onto the road at the end of the driveway. Abigail shifted the car into gear, stomped the gas, and watched Mrs. Harting stroll into the center of the road in her rearview mirror.

CHAPTER 16

ABIGAIL

The Honda shuttered as it rapidly decelerated and veered from the paved road into the gravel driveway. Abigail stopped abruptly beside the Whispering House and threw the car into park, her eyes glued to the unlit windows on the face of the house. She threw the driver's door open and stumbled around the back of the car to the porch steps on partially numb legs.

She crashed into the front door and fumbled in her pocket for the key.

"Got it."

The key dropped from her shaking hand to the wood floor.

"Damnit!"

She bent and snatched the key from the frigid porch floor. Her head swam as she stood and jammed the key into the lock.

She grabbed the doorknob and stopped. Her frantic breathing reflected from the door like a soft, warm breeze—like the house exhaling her fear back into her face.

"Please be anywhere but here."

Mrs. Harting's words echoed in her memory. *She needs you, Abigail. Go, now.*

Abigail pushed the door. Her heart lodged in her throat as the dark home took her in.

Anywhere but here.

As she stepped into the foyer and cleared the threshold, the doorknob slipped from her hand. The door slammed shut behind her, the aged hardwood door crashing into the hard, cold frame in a thunderous boom. Abigail flinched and lunged toward the sitting room to her right to avoid being hit. She caught herself in the archway and froze. A desperate groan crawled from her throat.

A casket stood prominently in the center of the sitting room. Decorative gold handles spanned the length of the polished rosewood coffin. A single starling stood on the lid like a sentry guarding a tomb.

The floor shifted underfoot. "I can't do this."

The sunlight penetrating the home's windows flickered like artificial lights on a temperamental switch, surged to painful brightness, then fled the sky outside. Night swallowed the earth.

Abigail's fingernails drew splinters of wood from the archway trim, and tears flooded her eyes in panicked streams.

A shadow emerged at the edge of the darkness. The sound of someone striking a match filled the room and light bloomed near the couch. Delilah emerged in candlelight, seated on the couch. She held a single candle in her black lace gloved hands. A sheer mourning veil hid her face.

"Take a seat, Abigail. This won't be easy for any of us."

"No, Mama!" Abigail burst into tears. "Please don't do this."

Delilah kept her eyes on the candle's dancing flame. "What's done is done, dear. It's time to restore our family."

Delilah tipped the candle and lit several others standing tall in a candelabra on the coffee table. The expanding candlelight revealed a room from another time, a childhood Abigail had relived in countless dreams. The framed portrait of Abigail's aunt Lydia and cousin Adeline rested upon the fireplace mantle. Armchairs sat in the corners to either side of the front windows. Everything appeared just as it had in 1966, the year which took everything.

Delilah's eyes shifted from the candles to the coffin. Tears shimmered on her lashes in the candlelight as she sighed under the weight of debilitating grief.

"Bring her to me."

The starling danced on the coffin.

CHIRP CHIRP CHIRP

The casket jumped on its stand as its inhabitant awoke. The sound of limbs pounding the lid interrupted the muffled cries of a hysterical voice.

"Stop!" Abigail screamed. She pried her shaking hands from the archway molding and stumbled toward the casket.

The starling danced and chirped on the pulsing lid, flapping its wings erratically.

CHIRP CHIRP CHIRP

Abigail reached for the bird, but it flew into the empty fireplace and disappeared up the flue. She nearly toppled the coffin as she collided with it. Acting on reflex, she hugged the coffin to prevent it from tipping over. Abigail's clothes clung to her body as liquid ran down her abdomen to her legs. Black water seeped from the closed lid.

Punching.

Kicking.

Drowning.

"Bring her to me!" Delilah yelled from the couch. Her sharp exclamation nearly blew out the candles, casting dancing shadows around the room.

Abigail hugged the lid to keep it closed. She pressed her body hard to its surface, absorbing the desperate strikes from the other side with her face and chest. She turned her head toward her mother and pleaded with her entire heart.

"I can't lose her. She can't be here. *Please.*"

Delilah calmly lifted one hand above the candelabra. "It's time to come home, Abigail." In one swift motion, she dropped her raised hand and snuffed out the candles. The room fell into total darkness.

Abigail's fingers lost their strength, and her hands slid from the coffin's handles. No longer held down, the coffin lid shot open, a torrent of water breaking free.

Constance emerged from the casket in a massive gasp.

Abigail tried to hug her, but Constance's flailing arms made it impossible. Water flew from her coughing mouth and doused Abigail. Seeing Constance in this room, in this state, made Abigail realize her mother was right. It was too late to turn back. With Constance now present and aware, there was nothing Abigail could do to stop the inevitable. She squeezed her eyes tight, laid her head on the closed lower half of the coffin, and wept. Abigail wept for her mother. She wept for her sister. She wept for her traumatic, pointless life.

"Abigail! Get me out of here!" Constance grabbed at Abigail's shirt in the dark. In an act of defiance and acceptance, Abigail retreated from her sister. She slid down the slick side of the casket to the floor, propping herself up on her exhausted, shivering arms.

In the windows behind the coffin, the morning sun pulled itself to the horizon, pushing a warm light into the room. A calmness forced its way into her core.

It's happening. Time is slipping. Mama has us.

Her mother sat upright like a statue on the couch. She no longer donned the mourner's veil. Instead, she wore a dark blue shirtwaist dress buttoned to the neck, and cinched at the waist by a thin brown belt. Her hair framed her face in cascading curls. Subtle makeup highlighted her youth and accentuated her slightly upturned nose, round eyes, and perfectly shaped lips. Three melted candles lay broken on the floor at her feet.

Knobby-kneed legs stretched out before Abigail. She was a child again, like she was during her last visit to the house. A new fear emerged in her gut.

What if Constance saw her like this? Would she understand this was some sort of dream or hallucination?

Black water dripped down the side of the coffin but left no trace on the polished, *not-charred*, hardwood floor. Two worlds met there, her reality and whatever this state was, but separated like oil and water. Above Abigail in the casket, Constance went silent.

"Mama? Abigail?" Constance leaned over the side of the coffin. Her mouth hung open in disbelief. Water dripped from her flawless, unscarred face. Abigail wept harder.

"Welcome home, baby." A smile spread across Delilah's shaking lips. She stood and crossed the room to the coffin.

From her spot on the floor, Abigail watched Constance abruptly turn and pull back in terror. The coffin rocked on the flimsy rack. Delilah held one hand out, and the coffin steadied.

The girls froze as Delilah reached them. Abigail's heart beat with so much conflicted emotion she thought it may burst in her chest. She sensed overwhelming love in their mother's presence again, but she was terrified of how Constance would respond.

"Don't fear me, Constance. We're the same."

Constance shook her head in disbelief. "But you're—"

"Dead. Yes."

"We are *not* the same," Constance said in a voice soaked in denial.

Delilah raised her hand again and the world went black.

CHAPTER 17

CONSTANCE

Constance opened her eyes to the backyard and squinted against the intense morning sun. Dew clung to the grass pressed between her toes. The ground warmed and comforted her feet, a summer grass, not the hard, frozen ground of an early winter morning.

Mama, Abigail, the coffin.

She slowly turned in place, as if suspended in the web of a dream, and found her sister standing within arm's reach behind her.

"Abigail." Her sister's name fell from her mouth in slurred syllables and soft edges, her tongue thick like spun cotton.

A butterfly landed on Abigail's shoulder and flexed its wings. Abigail smiled, momentarily relaxing the worried lines around her eyes.

Constance looked beyond their mother's perfectly kept garden to the house. Its bright white siding bit the nerves in her eyes. She squinted against the harsh glare, hoping to see their mother.

"I'm here," Delilah's voice settled into her right ear like a breeze.

Constance turned her head and saw her mother standing beside them in her blue shirtwaist dress. Had she been there this whole time?

"What's happening?" Constance muttered.

Delilah smiled, her eyes two shining diamonds in her beautifully tanned face. She raised her hand and pressed it to Constance's forehead.

"See."

Constance's vision left her in a blinding flash and an exhilarating rush of cool energy pulsed through her veins. A pinpoint of color emerged in the white, then slowly expanded like the opening aperture of a camera lens. For the first time since the fire, she saw herself as she was in her youth—unblemished, unscarred, and unaffected by flame.

She saw herself through her mother's eyes.

"See, Constance." Her mother's voice rang in her head rather than her ears. It came from, and remained, within. "We are here together. Just as we were. Just as we'll always be."

The cool sensation flowed from her in waves. She felt like she was standing naked in a morning breeze. Then, the brightness stole her vision from her again.

"Open your eyes."

Constance did as her mother commanded. She was back in her body, back on the web. She stood before her mother and sister in the dreamy embrace of the backyard. Despite Delilah's beaming smile, Abigail wore marks of dread upon her face. Her eyes fell at the edges and her lips pressed firm to suppress emotion.

Constance pulled her fingers across her smooth cheeks. She searched for scars but found none. Her lips were proportionate and her nose was full. "This must be a dream. I'm normal again. How is this possible?"

"You and me ... we've moved on from life."

"No." Constance took a step back and the world spun, threatening to topple her. "Tell her she's wrong, Abigail. Tell her we're dreaming. You aren't a teenager and I'm not dead."

Abigail said nothing as tears broke down her cheeks.

Constance looked back and forth between her mother and sister. Her pulse quickened with each passing second. "Why aren't you saying anything?"

Abigail wiped her face and drew a deep, shuddering breath. "She's right. You *are* the same. You're dead."

The world stood still in the wake of Abigail's words. Constance froze, unable and unwilling to accept what she'd heard.

"That isn't possible. You can't drown in a dream."

"You didn't drown. You burned. Twenty years ago."

"What are you talking about? I've lived with you for twenty–"

"As a ghost," Abigail interrupted her.

Constance took a step back from her sister and mother, refusing to believe.

"This is a dream. I fell asleep on the couch at home and I'm having a nightmare." Constance rubbed her hands on her forearms.

"No, you're here. This is real. You've walked alongside me for too long." Abigail closed her eyes and choked back her emotions. "Mama's right. It's time for you to come home."

Delilah stepped forward. "There's something I need to show you."

"I'm not going anywhere with you. I want to wake up and go home."

As the words left her mouth, Constance realized she couldn't see the place she called home in her mind. She squeezed her eyes shut and hoped to wake up, to recall the image of the couch in the living room. Nothing came. She couldn't remember a single detail of the place she'd called home for the past two decades.

All she remembered was pain. Being an outcast. Avoiding people. Hiding in plain view. Propping herself behind her sister and hoping to make it through each day.

She hadn't lived. She'd died in every way possible.

"Come with me." Delilah turned and walked across the yard.

"I'm so sorry I didn't tell you sooner," Abigail said, sniffling between words. "You seemed so happy, and I wasn't ready to let you go. Now, I don't have a choice." Abigail turned and followed their mother across the yard.

Constance stood firmly in place, refusing to follow them, refusing to believe. Reaching the edge of the yard, Delilah stopped in front of the shed and raised her right hand, her palm upturned to the sky.

"Come, Constance."

"I'm not–" Constance protested when Delilah dropped her hand and the world went black again.

This time, Constance experienced everything. Her body elevated and her mind scrambled as an external frequency jammed her thoughts. A gentle force moved her across the yard, her eyes fixed on the sky above, her arms and legs dangling out of reach of her mind. An intense *HUUUUM-MMMMM* vibrated through her body from head to toe, stimulating every nerve in a deep, thrumming energy. Lower, her feet touched soil again. Grounded, the frequency subsided and she regained her faculties.

She stood beside her mother a dozen paces from the closed shed doors. Abigail entered the frame and wiped tears from her childish face as she placed the other hand on the door. She stopped and looked back at Delilah. Their mother nodded, and Abigail pulled the doors open.

As the doors swung, a deep, calming shadow fell across the yard. The world changed around them, reminding Constance of when she'd witnessed a solar eclipse in her youth. A single starling flew from the peak of the house and disappeared into the shed's open mouth.

CHIRP CHIRP CHIRP

A pinpoint yellow light came alive in the shadows. Then another, and another. That one glowing more green than the last. One at a time, a swarm of lightning bugs came alive, illuminating the shed's interior.

In the center of the shed stood a solitary slab of stone. A headstone.

"Dear God." Constance read the inscription as the lightning bugs crawled along the words etched on the stone's face.

Constance Fairchild

February 1948 - November, 1966

True love is deeper than any grave.

Abigail turned at the edge of her sight. "It's time to take your wings."

Constance's feet lost their contact with the ground. Lifted again. Face pulled up to the sky. The sun eclipsed in a ring of fire.

Above the trees. Along the path. An airborne voyage to the forest cemetery.

Down. Down. Feet on the soil once again.

Constance lowered her eyes from the sky and settled them on the family cemetery. Trees enveloped them in a constricting circle. Familiar tombstones surrounded her. A few yards ahead, Delilah stood with her back turned to Constance. She raised her right arm, palm facing up toward the sky again.

"Come, Constance." She didn't fight the command this time. Besides, resistance was futile. Her mother had proven that several times already. She walked to Delilah's side and stood before her mother's grave.

"We rest together." Delilah lowered her arm and laced her fingers before her waist.

"Are you saying I'm ... buried with you?"

Delilah nodded. Abigail emerged from the path and walked over to them. She no longer appeared young.

"You came to my bedroom the night you died in the hospital. Earlier that day, the doctors told us you most likely wouldn't survive, and I knew they were right. I went to bed that night and prayed that you'd come to me if anything happened before the sun rose the next morning. I had faith you would. I've seen ghosts ever since I can remember. I've seen you every day since." She walked around the back of Delilah's headstone. "It was hard to navigate our time together without tipping you off. Your fear of this place helped quite a lot. You never asked to come visit Mama's grave, but we feared that one day, when we got older, you'd ask to come here. We couldn't let you see your gravestone, so we kept it in the shed to protect you from the truth."

"You lied to me," Constance said in a cold, hurt voice.

"I was afraid of losing you. And you needed me, so I kept the lie up as long as I could. I'm so sorry."

Anger approached Constance's heart, but fell away. Peace settled there instead. She could no longer fight the inevitable. Death had come for her so many years ago and she'd refused to recognize it. The time had finally come to let go. Overhead, the sun emerged from behind the moon, casting light across the treetops in an expanding arc. Delilah placed one hand on each daughter's shoulder.

"Welcome home, girls."

CHAPTER 18

ABIGAIL

Abigail took in the sights, sounds, and smells of the kitchen as she entered the house through the back door.

Warm cinnamon and apples. Buttered rolls. Lemon wood polish. A vase of freshly cut wildflowers sitting on the counter beside the basket of keys and loose papers. Three perfectly imperfect place settings, complete with white glass plates, mason jar drinking glasses, and silver cutlery, welcomed them into dining.

The surreal sights and smells of her childhood kitchen at dinner time anchored Abigail to the threshold of the back door. She hadn't known what to expect when they'd returned from the family cemetery, but this was a shocking, albeit welcome, surprise.

Her mother moved like a breeze between the stovetop and the counter, a graceful blur of productivity with a smile. Constance stood just inside the kitchenette, her eyes wide and weary. Constance had been through the ringer today. Abigail wasn't sure how much more she could take before something gave.

Abigail marveled at the sheer beauty of Constance's perfectly contoured face. The years had washed her memory of her sister's natural beauty. Although she'd seen her restoration earlier in the sitting room, she stared in awe as the hanging kitchen light illuminated Constance's newly restored face. Her deep blue eyes and tightly pressed lips gave up her secrets. Abigail saw fear and disbelief in those features. Constance looked like a teen model in the throes of existential crisis.

"Dinner will be ready in a few minutes. Take your seats, girls."

"But ..." Abigail's words trailed off into the room's viscous atmosphere. She blinked as if that would somehow clear the air. Her head floated with every cycle of her eyelids.

Things weren't this dreamy in the sitting room or in the backyard. What's happening?

"Don't 'but' me, young lady," Delilah feigned frustration, her smile giving away her true happiness. "Sit. You need your food."

Abigail turned her hands over, looking for trails or blurs at their edges. Her body seemed normal, but her thoughts were distant. Her mind flailed at the end of a ribbon a world away.

A set of wooden chair legs sliding across the hardwood floor pulled her ribbon tight and brought her back to the kitchenette. Constance had taken her seat at the table. She patted the seat beside her.

Sit down, Abi, Constance's voice entered through her thoughts instead of her ears.

"Okay," Abigail muttered and sat hard on the seat. "I feel weird."

"You need to eat, dear," Delilah said. She carried an empty serving platter with both hands and set it carefully in the center of the kitchen table.

"But the plate is empty," Abigail said.

Constance stared at her with slightly narrowed eyes. She looked confused.

"Stop being silly and eat up." Delilah stabbed at the platter with an oversized fork. Its metal tines rang a sharp report when they met the bare glass surface.

Constance's eyes dropped as her confusion morphed to concern. She leaned closer to Abigail. "Do you not see the chicken?"

Abigail looked up from the platter and shook her head. "I don't feel so good.".

Her mother suddenly appeared at her side and lay her hand on Abigail's shoulder. She stared into her mother's eyes, transfixed by the dark lines swirling in Delilah's corneas.

"You seem tired," Delilah said.

The daylight in the windows implied it was still early, but her brain said she'd stayed up all night. She looked for the clock on the wall above the trashcan and saw both hands steadily spinning backward. She looked back at the platter, now topped with a steaming pile of sliced chicken breasts. The smell reached her nostrils and turned her stomach into a tumbling knot.

"Wait. How did–?"

"There. That's better," Delilah said and took her seat beside Abigail. Her face glowed in the hanging light as the dark lines broke over the boundaries of her corneas and flooded the white of her eyes. "Dig in, girls."

CHAPTER 19

CONSTANCE

Constance watched Abigail's arms move like an automaton as she repeatedly cycled her empty fork between her plate and her mouth. Chicken spilled from her plate to the tablecloth.

It's like she can't see the food on her plate.

Constance looked past the light of the kitchen table into the hall leading to the front of the house. The recently polished floors reflected indirect sunlight from the rooms bordering the hall and foyer. The house looked and smelled freshly cleaned. Constance peered over her shoulder at the waning daylight in the backyard. Birds darted between the lawn and sky in an unpredictable rhythm. The trees and low brush at the edge of their property swayed in a light breeze.

"Well, that was yummy," Delilah said, drawing Constance's attention back to the trio at the table. Except Delilah wasn't in her seat. Constance spun in her chair. Their mother stood at the kitchen sink, wiping a plate dry as she stared out of the window.

Why is she drying plates?

Constance turned back to the table. Someone had removed all traces of their meal. Abigail had vacated her seat. She stood in front of the window at the end of the table.

"What do I do, Constance?" Her sunken eyes exposed her concern. "Do I stay?"

Delilah continued at the sink, as if she hadn't heard the question. "The clouds are moving in. We're in for another moonless night." A ripple moved across Delilah's face, a subtle wave shifting her features in a single pass. She dried her hands on the towel hanging below the sink. Delilah's shadow swung around her feet in an arc like the time-lapsed sundial. The shadow reached the counters, stopped, then shortened before climbing up Delilah's legs and back. Darkness settled around her in a black halo.

Delilah's eyes flashed light, then dark, her mouth quivering in a faltering smile.

"You girls need to get ready for bed. Who's bathing first?"

"Mama ... what's happening?"

Delilah held her composure as the shadow swelled and contracted around her. "Whatever do you mean, Constance?"

Constance looked back at Abigail standing at the window. Her sister's uneasy expression confirmed they were on the same page.

"The house, dinner, your shadow. I'm concerned about you."

"There's no reason to be concerned. We're finally home again. What's wrong with having a nice meal together?"

Constance mulled over her response before speaking. Abigail came to her side and placed her hand on the back of Constance's chair to show support.

"Mom, this feels like a dream. But something's wrong. I can't think clearly and my stomach is upset," Abigail said.

Delilah looked out of the sink window at the diminishing daylight. The smile fell from her face and a concerned intensity glowed in her slack cheeks and radiant eyes. "We've just had a long, eventful day. That's all. A good night's sleep will make a world of difference." Her voice trailed off. "Growing girls need their sleep."

Constance and Abigail exchanged a troubled look. Growing girls? Their mother spoke as if they were children.

This time, Abigail spoke up. "Mom, why don't you get some rest? We want to stay up and talk awhile."

Delilah's head whipped from the window. Her eyes regained clarity as they darted between the girls' faces. "That's fine, but I want you in your rooms. Do you hear me?"

A frigid wave passed over Constance as she processed her mother's stern words. Abigail tapped her shoulder, prompting her to rise from the table and follow her out of the kitchenette.

"Yes, ma'am." Constance pushed her chair back. This time, the legs made no sound on the floor. She stood in one effortless motion, her body numb and light. Staring down at her hands on the table, her breath caught in her chest. She couldn't feel the table. Her sister's hand moved from her shoulder. She saw it, felt nothing.

Ghosts don't feel, she thought. Then, without considering her words, Constance said, "That's not true."

"What's not true?" Delilah asked.

Constance sighed and shook her head. "Nothing. Come on, Abi."

The girls walked down the short hall, Abigail leading the way. As they reached the stairs, Constance became increasingly nervous. Abigail must have shared her concern because she stopped at the bottom step and shot a look over her shoulder at Constance.

"Maybe we should just go to the family room." Abigail said.

Constance looked past her sister, up into the dark open mouth of the stairwell. She placed one foot on the first step and paused. These stairs led to their rooms, rooms they hadn't seen in twenty years. Rooms where they'd slept and dreamed and laughed. A memory surfaced in Constance's mind of Abigail, seated in her closet before a makeshift altar. Another came of her reading Uncle Wade's letter in her mother's bedroom and the cold wave she'd experienced before going numb in the kitchenette returned. Dancing pinpricks graced her arms and neck. She squeezed her eyes shut and imagined Uncle Wade screaming at the bedroom window as he watched Lydia march to her death across the backyard.

And, of course, there was the bathroom tub, and all the horror it held but could not wash from their lives.

Constance opened her eyes. "We'll go to your room."

CHAPTER 20

ABIGAIL

Abigail and Constance stood in her empty childhood bedroom. Outside the window, the sun slowly fell behind the trees across the street. Sounds of their mother moving about the kitchen downstairs carried through the old wood floor beneath their feet. Despite the odd experience of being in her former bedroom, Abigail felt safe discussing plans and concerns with Constance in seclusion upstairs. Her senses were hyper-sharp. She forgave herself for being on edge. Anyone would get anxious under these conditions. This house gave the dead a place to live. A place in a traumatic, violent time.

"So, where do we start?" Constance asked.

"I'm not sure whether I should stay the night or go home," Abigail deflected to avoid explaining her unease. "I'm worried about you and Mama. What if I leave and come back to an empty house? What if something happens to you while I'm gone and I lose you forever?"

Constance stood where Abigail's bed used to sit. The room looked so much smaller than Abigail remembered, even without the furniture to border its walls and fill its center with the plush comforts of a young teen's life. Constance looked past her to the open hall. "I'm not going anywhere."

"You say that. But how do you know? You just found out you're a ghost a few hours ago. How can you be confident in anything right now?"

Constance didn't seem to take offense. How could she?

"Look, you've got a life to live. You can't just stay here and avoid the bookstore, the house, and your friends. Those things make your life what it is. I hate to say it, but that's over for me now." Sadness settled into Constance's voice as she admitted the finality of her situation. "This is what I have now. I'll stay here with Mama. You go home and get a good night's sleep. Wake up tomorrow and go to work, and when you're done, close the store, grab some dinner, and meet us here."

The room grew darker as the light drained from the windows behind Constance. Abigail turned her ear toward the hallway, the stairs, and the sound of their mother opening and closing the cabinets downstairs. The distraction gave her time to contemplate how she'd arrange staying overnight in the house.

"I'm not talking about moving in permanently. Just tonight."

"You aren't serious. You can't stay here."

"Why not?" Abigail asked. "I'm not afraid of staying here with you two."

Constance paced the room. "Didn't you say you felt weird during dinner?"

"Well, yeah, but I'm better now. When I'm that close to Mama, she has power, and it's intoxicating. She makes me feel odd. That's all. I'll be fine."

"No, you won't be fine. I'm not convinced that's Mama you're feeling." Constance turned from her and opened the closet doors.

"What do you mean?"

"Nothing. Go home tonight and come back tomorrow. I promise we'll be here."

"You're hiding something from me. What is it?"

"I'm not hiding anything."

"Well, what aren't you telling me?"

Constance lowered her voice. "I felt odd too, but not in the same way. It's not just because you're alive and we're dead. There's something around Mama, like a shadow.

That's what's interfering with us. It's keeping us from seeing her clearly."

Abigail's face tightened with confusion. She thought about what she'd seen in the kitchen, but couldn't recall a shadow on their mother. She remembered the scene like a strange dream. However, the dream wasn't beautiful like her previous experiences with their mother earlier in the week.

"I sensed it. I just didn't see it. But that doesn't mean it's not there. I've seen ghosts my whole life, but I've never seen a shadow or a darkness around a ghost like you're describing."

"Not to discount your gift, or curse, or whatever you consider it, but you aren't one of us. You may see us, but you aren't one of us. It's possible we see things you can't." Constance took her by the wrists. "You're not safe. You need to leave."

Abigail pulled away from Constance with little resistance. "Well, if I'm not safe now, what changes tomorrow? You and I have been together all this time without a problem. You're just trying to keep me from this house. I get it, you don't trust it. But I told you, I'm fine."

Constance stood taller and crossed her arms. "We don't know what we're talking about, Abi. Neither of us. This is all new. Even though I've been dead and living with you this whole time, we weren't *here*. We weren't with *her*. We haven't experienced this house together until now. You came here earlier, without me, and nothing happened to you. I wonder if me being here with you makes things different."

Guilt set into Abigail's skin like a warm balm. Constance had unknowingly revealed Abigail's lie. Something *had* happened to her. Her time alone with Delilah had been beautiful and terrifying, but somehow comfortable and addictive. The experience hadn't repelled her. Rather, it pulled her past logic and honesty. She couldn't resist it.

Maybe Constance was right. Perhaps things were different when they were together in the house. Perhaps she could experience things Abigail couldn't.

No. Abigail didn't want to believe that. She wanted to believe she could stay with them. That she could see them as they saw each other. Being together with her family was all she ever wanted.

"You know I've got nothing if I don't have you." Her voice quivered on the verge of crying. "I can't deal with losing you. I believed I'd lost you once, and it scared me to death. It was hard enough trying to get over losing Mama, but then I had to face losing you. But you didn't leave, and I swore I would never let you go again. Now you're aware of your death, and I'm terrified that you're going to move on."

"Abi, I'm not–"

"What happens to me if you cross over while I'm gone? What if you cross fully into death and I'm left here alone?"

Constance paused, likely contemplating Abigail's words. "Well, Mama's still here, and she's been gone over twenty years, so what makes you think I'll cross over against my will?"

Abigail didn't have an answer for that.

"I wonder if she's been here since her death," Constance continued. "What if she's been waiting for us? She needs our help. Whatever that shadow is, it might hurt her."

"What if it's not a shadow?" Abigail asked, "What if it's part of her? What if the shadow you see *is* her?"

Constance shook her head. "No. It doesn't feel like her. It's like something completely separate. More like a spirit, like a darkness clinging to her."

Initially, Abigail hadn't taken Constance's claims seriously. Now, she considered the hypothesis with dread.

"What if it's using her like a puppet to get to you?"

Constance had finally exposed her genuine concern.

"Me?" Abigail asked, honestly surprised. "Why me?"

"Well, you're still alive." Constance's words hung in the air between them like an unopened prize on the end of a string. That was the undeniable truth and risk at play, wasn't it? Abigail worried Constance was using this to play into her fears.

"You don't know that. You don't know if that makes me more vulnerable than you." Sadness and frustration collided in Abigail's heart. "You don't know if your death makes you or Mama safe, or puts me in danger. We know nothing."

"Yeah, but what can it do to me?" Constance interrupted. "I'm already dead. You're the only thing I have to lose. So we're not exactly in the same boat here. Look out for yourself. Don't worry about us. We're already gone."

"No, you're not," Abigail snapped. "You're here. I'm looking at you. We had dinner with Mama–"

Constance interrupted, now more upset. "*Did* we eat dinner with Mama, or did we eat dinner with whatever that is surrounding her? You're not safe here. You're not staying tonight."

This was all too much for Abigail. The idea of leaving and going back to her boring life without Constance terrified her.

Abigail closed the distance between them. "Come with me back to the house. At least then, if there *is* something dangerous here, I'll know you're safe."

"You want me to leave her here alone with that thing?" Constance asked. "No way."

"But if it can hurt her, you might be in danger," Abigail pleaded.

"I'm not going with you," Constance spoke sternly. "I don't belong there." She raised her hands, palms open, tears streaming down her beautiful, supple cheeks. She dropped her hands in frustration. "Mama and I probably shouldn't be here either. Maybe if we move on, it will finally end this curse that's torn my life apart and I can find peace."

Abigail's heart broke into a pile of delicate, wounded flesh. "Don't say that."

"Listen to me, Abi. Live a life for me. Do the things I can't do. Get the hell out of this town. Go start your life somewhere else. Sell the bookstore. Move on. You could–"

Abigail cut her off. "Without you, I've got nothing, just a failing book store in a town that doesn't want one. Without you, there's nothing. I'm staying."

"And exactly how do you suppose that would work?" Constance asked. "Are we just gonna make our imaginary beds and take a bath in that goddamn tub? Is that what we're gonna do? We're just gonna live like we used to, wake up in the morning and Mama will make us breakfast and we'll clean the house all day? That's crazy. You're not making any sense."

"Well, I don't want to be alive then." Abigail sobbed, heavy grief crushing her. The tragedy of Constance's death all those years ago opened fresh wounds in her again.

"I can't do this without you. I won't. I'd rather be dead than alone."

They stood in silence for a moment, Constance wiping her face with her palms and Abigail staring at her shoes in shame.

"Never say that again," Constance said. "You need to see how good you've got it. Mama and I have nothing."

"Well, you've got each other," Abigail replied. "And if you cross over, you'll see everyone we've lost. Aunt Lydia, Adeline, Uncle Wade, everybody. There's no one left here for me."

Constance took her wrists again. "Listen to me. Let's do this one day at a time. You go home tonight. Shower, sleep, go to work tomorrow, and then come back and *I promise* I'll be here for you. I won't leave. Do this for me."

Abigail wiped her face and drew a shaky breath. "Fine, I'll go." She turned and exited her empty bedroom with no more argument.

Constance followed her out of the room and down the stairs. They stepped softly to avoid alerting their mother to Abigail's departure. Abigail grasped the front doorknob and something shifted around her. She glanced down the hall.

"Let's go, girls," Delilah called from the kitchen.

Abigail fixed Constance with her eyes and spoke low. "If you're gone when I come back tomorrow, I'll kill myself." She opened the door and left. As her back foot crossed the threshold, the door closed behind her, vacuum tight, sealing everything within it from the outside world.

CHAPTER 21

CONSTANCE

Temporarily relieved, Constance watched Abigail leave through the front door. She stood in the foyer with her face in her shaking hands, paralyzed with concern for her sister and indecision about how to handle her mother. What should she do now? She sensed a primal need to protect Abigail by sending her away, but she knew her sister was vulnerable alone in her current state. Then there was their mother. Constance assumed the shadow she saw around her was bad, but she needed to confirm her suspicion.

"Girls?" Delilah's concerned voice came from the hall behind her. Constance dropped her hands from her face.

What if she hears Abigail's car and tries to stop her from leaving?

Constance hurried down the hall toward her mother. When she entered the empty kitchenette, she saw Abigail opening her car door through the side window. Abigail disappeared from view and the car's engine roared to life. As its headlights came alive, Delilah's voice came from somewhere behind her.

"Constance?" Urgent footfalls moved down the stairs to the hall behind her.

She was in the kitchen last I saw her. When did she pass me and go upstairs?

"I'm here, Mama," Constance called.

Delilah emerged from where the hall met the kitchenette. She'd changed into flannel pajamas and put her hair up in a loose bun. Her shadow remained dark and pulsing. Smoke-like tendrils licked the air around her as she swayed in place in the opening. Her eyelids rapidly blinked as she scanned the room. "Where is your sister going? She's not leaving, is she? It's not safe out there."

"She's fine. Abi can't stay tonight. She has to work tomorrow, but she'll be back."

Delilah winced. "Work? The girl doesn't have a job. She's twelve years old." She seemed genuinely confused.

"She'll come back tomorrow. I promise."

Delilah ignored her plea and turned for the front door. She took a single step and, acting on instinct, Constance reached for her shoulder. Her fingers breached the darkness rolling from her mother's body. The shadow seeped into Constance's bare skin and her vision broke into a million black squares before she realized she could no longer see.

Constance opened her eyes to nearly complete darkness. She smelled bleach and porcelain cleaner and her fingers rested on the edges of a porcelain sink.

She was in the hall bathroom.

Two incandescent bulbs flanking the mirror above the sink slowly came to life, casting drab light to the stark white tile floor and walls. The clawfoot tub appeared directly ahead. Delilah stood beside the tub, her expressionless face staring down into the empty basin. Through the dim light, Constance faced her reflection in the mirror. Her skin hung loose on her once beautiful face. Her right eye drooped slightly, and her mouth turned down on the same side. Yellowing, waxy skin spanned the entirety of her head from her hairline to her neck in a progressing state of decay. She tried to pry her eyes from the mirror but couldn't. Her hands gripped the sink so hard she feared it may shatter and slice her palms to shreds.

"Mama ... what's ... happening?" Constance mumbled through pressed, immovable lips.

"'The water runs black before the gate," her mother said from just outside her vision. Constance wanted to look, but she couldn't pry her eyes from her decomposing face in the mirror.

"She needs us," Delilah said in a slurred voice. "She needs us here."

"Who needs us? Are you talking about ...?"

The mirror darkened and Constance's head whipped to the right under the influence of an unseen force. A distressed groan rattled in Delilah's throat as she bent her knees and kneeled on the tile floor beside the tub.

"She needs us." Delilah reached into the tub and pressed a tapered, off-white plug into the drain. Then she reached for the faucet valves with one hand. The valve stems squealed with the turn of the handles.

Black water cascaded from the faucet and swirled in the stopped tub.

Delilah's face turned toward Constance, the low light disguising the details of her mother's face. Constance watched the charcoal gray shadow clinging to her arms shed and mix with the black water building in the tub.

"She needs us."

Constance wanted to run. She wanted to be anywhere but in that poorly illuminated bathroom on the edge of the afterlife. She closed her eyes and imagined Abigail driving home, away from the danger, far from this nightmare, lifetimes away from this cursed place. She cried out to her across the chasm.

"Stay away, Abi. This place is dangerous. This place is death."

Surely if her sister returned, she would die here. Constance knew that in her heart.

Constance's eyes pried open, one at a time. The water now filled half the tub. The black liquid pitched back and forth like water sloshing in a rocking ship. Delilah raised her hand and the water pouring from the spout stopped.

Constance stood rigid like a statue just three feet away and utterly helpless to act.

"We have to go. I have to take you away from here," Delilah droned.

Oh, God no. This can't be happening. Not now. Not like this.

Constance choked back a scream as she watched a small porcelain face emerge from the black water.

"Adeline?"

Adeline's eye snapped open on her milky white face, and the room grew entirely silent. Then she disappeared below the water in a rapid jerking motion and the violent thrashing began.

Inside, Constance flew into an ungoverned panic. She stood paralyzed and at the complete mercy of the scene playing out before her. Water flew from the tub, splattering the walls with dissimilarly sized black dots. Streaks ran down the tub sides and puddled on the floor around Delilah's legs. Constance tried to scream, to beg for Delilah to save the girl, but her mouth would not move and her voice refused to come forth.

Kneeling beside the tub, Delilah remained calm, her head bowed like clergy at the altar. She ran her hands along the sides of the tub as if to steady the vessel berthing death into the bathroom for the thousandth time. She looked at Constance and mouthed the words, *she needs us.*

The thrashing stopped.

Delilah planted her palms on the tub and pressed as she stood. As if attached by strings, Adeline's body rose from the murky water in unison with Delilah. Water ran from the girl's pale white body and cotton dress as she came to her full height before Constance. Amazingly, her dress bore no stains from the water. Delilah smiled and held out one hand to steady Adeline as she stepped from the tub.

"Hello, Constance." The honey in her youthful voice released Constance from her paralysis. "I can't imagine how you feel. I'm sorry if I scared you."

"I don't understand what's happening. I mean, I know you drowned here, in this tub, and you haunted the house all those years ago. But I didn't know you still came back."

"I came back for *you*," Adeline replied.

Constance stepped back and sensed the closed door at her back. Should she flee? *Could* she flee? She wasn't sure leaving the house was an option for her anymore. She needed to face this head on.

Adeline looked Delilah over before turning her attention back to Constance.

"She needs us." This time, Adeline said the words. Delilah couldn't have possibly been referring to herself when she'd repeated that phrase earlier, could she?

"Why? What's happening?"

"It's our time," Delilah answered. "It's time to go home." The room tightened around them. Constance couldn't go now. Abigail may do the unthinkable if they left.

"No. We can't go yet. We can't leave Abigail alone." Constance pleaded.

"Abigail ..." Delilah's thoughts trailed off again. "Where is your sister?"

Adeline reached up and closed both Delilah's eyelids with one gentle swiping motion. Delilah fell silent and her arms went slack, hanging loose from her shoulders. The black cloud around her thinned into a barely perceptible haze.

"You can fix her?" Constance asked.

"No. I can only help her for a short time. She's haunted by the darkness in this house. It's evil and it'll take her, then come for you next. You need to cross over and leave this place." Adeline's voice grew harder. "You aren't safe here, Constance. None of us are. But your mother refuses to cross over without you and your sister."

"What am I supposed to do?" Constance had the answer, but felt helpless. She'd made a promise to Abigail, and she intended to keep it as long as she could.

"Of course it's not Abigail's time yet. But your mother will go if you're with her. And without you two here, Abigail won't have a reason to return."

"You don't understand. If we leave, Abigail will kill herself. You can't expect me to risk that."

Constance saw Delilah's eyes were open again. Her heart collapsed at the thought of her mother hearing her predict her sister's suicide.

"She would never–" Delilah started.

"She would," Constance interrupted.

"You're wrong. Abigail would never do such a thing. She's just a girl." Delilah's mouth worked to contain her escalating emotions. "Besides, we could always come back to see her."

Their eyes fell to the tub, and its horrid black water still moving unnaturally about the basin.

"I'm not ready. I don't trust any of this. I need to stay with my sister. I need time to figure this out." Constance reached behind her for the doorknob, but stopped. She had an obligation to help her mother as well, not to abandon her in a moment of fear and doubt.

"Go without me. I'll stay here with Abigail until it's time for us to cross over together."

"No way. I won't leave without you girls," Delilah replied.

"You don't have much longer," Adeline said to Delilah. "You've been here far too long. The darkness is hurting you. We can see it, even if you can't." Adeline turned her head to Constance. "This house is sour. The dead can't exist here for long without harm. Keep Abigail away from the dark spirit in these walls or it'll do to her what it did to you. It will *kill* her."

"What spirit? Do you know who it is?" Constance asked. Delilah's shadow hummed like a tuning fork being struck. Her eyes rolled back and her knees buckled. Adeline and Constance grabbed her by the arms to keep her upright.

"It's happening to you, too." Adeline looked down at Constance's arm. A small, dark film blurred the interface of her pale skin and the surrounding surfaces. A new fear settled on Constance like a lead weight.

"Settle matters with your sister. You go home tomorrow night."

CHAPTER 22

ABIGAIL

"Shut up. I'm not listening to this anymore." Abigail clenched the steering wheel, glancing over at Steph, the dead teen who had appeared at the stoplight at the intersection of Route 60 and Rochambeau. Steph had refused to stop talking, and Abigail felt like another word might send her over the edge.

"Ignore me if you want, but it won't change things. I need you to listen." Stephanie Silvera persisted.

They'd hung out in gym class in eleventh grade, but a drunk driver had put an end to Stephanie on a random Saturday evening in January 1970. In fact, the accident happened at the very intersection where Steph had appeared in the car. Another life ended far too soon. Another ghost left to wander their town in search of resolution.

These days, Abigail occasionally saw Steph outside her parents' house on the way into work. Her mother, kneeling in the flower bed beside the steps to their colonial style home, turned soil and yanked weeds as her daughter's ghost watched from the front step, her skull breached and brain slick and glistening in the summer sun.

"I'm not getting in the habit of talking to ghosts," Abigail said as she checked her side mirror and merged into the left lane. "Besides, it's not true. Constance promised."

"Promises are meant to be broken. Just like rules." Blood dripped from the girl's open head to the center console.

TAP TAP TAP TAP

"You really screwed up, Abi. I hope you realize that. You had them. All you had to do was stay with them in the house. They'll be gone when you go back tomorrow."

Abigail squeezed the cold steering wheel. Her knuckles glowed in the moonlight streaming through the windshield. She cranked the heat another notch and watched the dashed lines in the road zip by at the edge of her headlights. The car's cold interior chilled her hands and feet. Not that she cared. Discomfort was the last thing on her mind. She had frustration and anger to warm her core and exhaustion to distract her from worry. The lingering fog of her time in the house sapped the clarity from her mind and the energy from her limbs like a hangover.

"You belong with them at the Whispering House. There's nothing for you out here. This is temporary, anyway. All of it. The cars, the houses, the relationships, the jobs; all temporary. And pointless. What's the point if you die in the end? Or in the middle, for that matter. You're in the middle now, right?"

Abigail squinted hard to clear her tired eyes. *Ignore her.*

"How is it that so much time has passed since I died and we're essentially still the same? No marriage. No kids. No hope. It's sad, really."

"At least I can hug your parents if I want," Abigail said in a harsh, low voice.

"Ditto. I'll tell your dad you said hi," Steph countered. "It's been a while since you saw him, huh? Didn't he abandon you guys?"

Abigail turned the radio on and twisted the knob hard to the right. "Alive and Kicking" from Simple Minds blared through the speakers so loudly Abigail felt the treble in her teeth. She didn't miss the irony of the song title. She turned to yell triumphantly over the music, "Did you hear that? Alive and kicking. Ha!" but Steph was no longer with her.

"That'll be ten dollars and twenty-five cents."

As Abigail fished in her pocket for exact change, the disinterested cashier scratched his chest and looked to the ceiling, clearly ready to end his shift. RediMart was particularly quiet that night. Abigail had stopped for gas and a bottle of Coke before heading home to heat a gourmet dinner of chicken noodle soup and a grilled cheese sandwich.

"Here you go." Abigail handed the unfolded ten-dollar bill, two dimes, and a nickel to the cashier, who took the money and deposited it in the register without making eye contact.

"Do you need a bag?"

"No."

"Have a good night."

"You too." Abigail exhaled her response before pushing her way through the glass door and into the rapidly cooling night. She'd overheard the cashier and an old man in line before her talk about the potential for snow in the coming days. She wasn't too concerned, but she sighed, knowing the entire town would shut down if as little as a dusting settled on the roads. Any inclement weather would keep people home, and that didn't bode well for book selling.

Maybe that's not such a bad thing. I could spend more time with Constance and Mama and not feel guilty, she thought as she crossed the illuminated sidewalk under buzzing fluorescent lights. She peeked through the windshield. The passenger seat was empty. No Steph to keep her company the rest of the way home.

Lucky me.

She got into the car and set her soda on the passenger seat.

"I told you she needed you," Mrs. Harting said from the backseat.

Abigail's heart jumped into her throat in surprise. She glanced into the rearview mirror to see the elder woman looking out the side window. Pearl earrings dangled from her stretched earlobes to match her pearl necklace and bracelet. She wore a baby blue pillbox hat with a broad bow on its side and a pair of matching gloves. Mrs. Harting was all dressed up for a night on the town.

"What is this? Is my car a therapist's couch for the deceased tonight?" Abigail blindly cranked the ignition and threw the car in reverse. Mrs. Harting sat quietly as Abigail backed out and put the car in drive.

"Is it okay to talk now?" the old lady asked.

"I guess. I mean, it's not like I can stop you anyway." Abigail felt more helpless than usual tonight in her dealings with the dead.

"I'm sorry you're having such a hard time tonight, dear. You know this will only get worse, right?"

"What will? The number of nosy ghosts visiting me tonight? Is the ghost of Christmas Yet to Come visiting next?"

"I'm not sure what you're talking about, Abigail. I don't know anyone with that title."

"I was being sarcastic. You know, Ebenezer Scrooge? A Christmas Carol?"

Mrs. Harting looked out the window, clutching her handbag in her lap as the moonlight striped her face in flashes through the passing trees.

"Are you going home?"

"Yep."

"Aren't you lonely there?"

Abigail took a deep breath and controlled her frustration. "I'm tired. I'm going to eat and go straight to bed."

"How can you think about sleeping at a time like this?" Mrs. Harting's face stayed glued to the window.

"Easy. I'm exhausted. Now, I'm not trying to be rude, but I'd prefer to be alone tonight, Mrs. Harting."

"Right, dear. Alone, just like every other night. Doesn't loneliness get old after a while? You should turn around and go back to Constance and your mother. They may still be there."

Abigail stared in the rearview mirror, scanning the old lady's face for hints of intent. Nothing.

"May?"

"Well, there's no telling. They could cross over at any time. It sure would be a shame if you never saw them again. Could you imagine? What a tragedy that would be." The old woman shook her head in apparent disappointment.

"I'm not doing this all night." Abigail had an edge in her voice now. "They'll be fine. I'll be fine. There's always tomorrow."

"Ha! Tomorrow. That's a hoot. I promise you with great confidence that we can never guarantee tomorrow. Especially in your state."

Abigail didn't like that statement one bit. She felt her cheeks warming as her pulse quickened.

"And what state am I in?" she asked.

"You're pathetic and vulnerable. You can see it if you look hard enough."

Abigail sat, stunned. In all the years she'd seen Mrs. Harting, she'd been nothing short of polite. She sounded completely out of character while dishing out harsh insults from the backseat. Her fingers tumbled over each other on her handbag as she spoke.

"Look closely and you'll see it on your edges. You've got a new darkness to you. It makes you ugly. And ignorant. You're just an ignorant, ruined shell. The darkness is a parasite, siphoning your life while you stumble home unaware. Look for yourself if you don't believe me."

Abigail stared hard at her face in the rearview mirror, but only found tired eyes donning puffy bags as ornaments. Her skin looked dry and scaly, her lips wrinkled and chapped. Her nose was still red from being outside at the gas station, but her pitching eyelids were the most troubling–

"Don't wreck, you moron."

Abigail pulled her eyes from the rearview mirror just in time to see the Honda's nose veer toward the shoulder as a turn presented itself ahead. She pulled the car back into the lane and looked in her rearview mirror again, this time to make sure no one following her saw her swerving. The last thing she needed tonight was an encounter with the police. She was too tired to master a sobriety test.

"I should have let you run off the road. Maybe then we could cut this unnecessary delay and get you back to your mother pronto." Mrs. Harting sounded like an entirely different person now. "You could've dodged the uncomfortable decision of dragging a blade across your wrist or swallowing a fistful of pills tonight. Oh well, I guess you'll just have to do the dirty work."

Abigail's pulse quickened. She'd stayed calm to this point, but Mrs. Harting broke through with that last statement. Her grim proclamation not only scared Abigail, it also enticed her. She'd promised Constance that she'd stay safe tonight, but sometimes it was better to ask for forgiveness than permission, right?

Stop thinking like that. What the hell is wrong with you?

"You're not real. And I'm not buying your darkness bullshit. I'm going home and getting my night over with so I can get tomorrow started. Now, kindly get lost."

Mrs. Harting smiled big. "I'm real, honey. And I'm not selling anything. The darkness you wear will grow thick and unavoidable. You'll see. Your cancer will consume, then kill you. You're totally fucked."

Someone driving in the opposite direction flashed their lights to warn her about a cop ahead or some road hazard she'd yet to encounter. When she looked in the backseat, Mrs. Harting was gone.

By the time Abigail finished chewing the last bite of her grilled cheese sandwich, she started nodding off at the small kitchen table. She desperately needed a shower before climbing into bed, but she wasn't convinced she'd make it. The ticking of the kitchen clock coaxed her into action. The sooner she got to bed, the better.

She carried her plate and bowl to the kitchen sink and flipped on the hot water. After rinsing the dishes, she added a few drops of soap to a wet dishrag and ran it across their surfaces. Good enough. She turned off the water and kept her tired eyes down to avoid the offensive light over the sink as she dried the dishes. She noticed her shadow trailed a step out of sync with her arm's movement.

She stopped. Her shadow fell into line on the counter below her arm. She blinked her eyes and looked around the room, inspecting the dark corners wrapping the sides of the table legs, chairs, and various jars on the counter.

No movement. She thought her exhaustion must be influencing her sight.

"The darkness you wear will grow thick and unavoidable," Mrs. Harting's words rebounded in her memory. *"You're totally fucked."*

Abigail flipped off the sink light and walked to the bathroom. She considered showering in the dark to avoid the harsh lights over the mirror. Maybe she'd shower with the hall light on and the door open instead.

Not after the day she'd had. No way.

She sucked it up, squinted, and turned on the bathroom lights. Moving quickly, she reached through the shower curtain and turned the water on. A hard spray of frigid water rained from the shower head to the tub basin. She shed her clothes to the floor beside the tub, then bent to pick them up and drop them in the square hamper across from the toilet. Motion in the mirror over her left shoulder arrested her movement.

Abigail whipped around, awkwardly exposed to whatever was moving behind her, and found nothing. She covered her breasts with one arm and approached the mirror. She locked the closed door–just in case. Her smooth, bare shoulders, chest, and stomach presented no abnormalities in her reflection. Steam floated in a light cloud above her head. The shower water must have finally warmed up.

Movement in the mirror again.

Abigail's eyes snapped left to the edge of the reflection to see a gray tendril roll from her shadow to the air and dissipate into the steam.

"The darkness you wear..."

Abigail's skin broke out in a wave of goosebumps. She rushed through the hanging shower curtain and into the scalding water. She flinched in pain, reached around the stream, and lowered the water temperature. Her motor skills askew, she fumbled for the washcloth and the slick bar of soap stuck to the tile soap tray. The water temp became more bearable. She closed her eyes and tried to steady her sudden panic as she soaped the cloth. Rubbing vigorously, the water stung her forearms as her mind replayed images of the dark gray tendril escaping her shadow to join the air above her head. The water soaked her hair and wrapped its liquid fingers around her neck. Abigail opened her eyes.

Blood ran into the drain at her feet. *A lot* of blood. It poured down her forearms. Her wrists looked scratched and mauled. Her fingers flew open and tossed the washcloth and soap. Instead, her razor left her hand. Its heavy faux wood handle rang a sharp report as it struck the porcelain beneath the bloody flow.

When did I grab a razor?

The drain made a hungry, desperate slurping sound as the flow of blood intensified.

Abigail flew out of the shower, her wet feet slipping across the slick tile floor. She collapsed into the wall and grabbed her towel hanging from the hook closest to the shower. She pressed the towel to her right wrist first, then pulled it back to see how badly she'd cut herself. The crater she'd apparently carved in her wrist ran jagged from wrist bone to wrist bone, an open smile full of bloody, meaty gums.

"Jesus Christ!" She inspected her left wrist and found it in better shape despite the beads of blood seeping from the deep scratches running up and down her forearm.

She didn't do this. She'd grabbed the washcloth and soap, not the razor.

"I tried to warn you, dear."

Abigail spun around and found Mrs. Harting standing in the open shower. Steaming hot water blasted the woman and soaked through her clothes. She clutched her bag in her two gloved hands. Water deflected from the sides of her pillbox hat.

"You're fucked."

Abigail ran naked and screaming from the bathroom.

CHAPTER 23
CONSTANCE

Constance opened her eyes to the star-mottled night sky. The unnaturally large winter moon hovered in the treetops to her right as her feet carried her down the path to the family cemetery.

Ahead of her, Adeline walked down the same path. A soft glow framed the girl, partially illuminating the encroaching grass at her feet.

"Wait, we can't go yet," Constance's voice left her lips and met soft resistance like a plea whispered into a pillow.

Adeline kept her pace and raised her right hand. She waved them on, imploring Constance to trail her without further objection. Conflicted emotions welled in Constance. Fear, frustration, hesitation, relief—she possessed all in equal measure.

The surrounding trees stole her breath with their beauty. Tall, bare at the trunk but lush at the canopy, she'd seen them a hundred times but never so uniform and spellbinding. They coaxed her with their swaying. Deep in their midst, shapes danced and flitted between each towering tree. Some wore gentle light, like fairies in a classic tale, others merely wore dark shrouds, their shapes their only evidence.

"What are they?"

"We're on the edge," Adeline replied. "The woods hold the spirits of those who aren't ready for the finality of death."

"You mean they're spirits who haven't crossed over?"

"Yes, but it's complicated. Some aren't worthy."

"What do you mean? Like sinners not allowed through the gates of heaven?" Constance feared Adeline's answer.

She shook her head. "Not quite. Some spirits aren't finished here. They hold their earthly relationships too tightly, their sins, their guilt. Some stay to watch after others. Others simply aren't willing to see their future."

The impact of Adeline's words burrowed into her heart. Was she passively warning Constance not to stay? Would death cast her to the woods if she refused to crossover?

"What about the house, then? Why does Mama get to stay there?" Constance saw the cemetery looming ahead over Adeline's shoulder. "Why am I not there?"

"Spirits can move between the edge and their lives. But unlike the others, she can't see the edge. The darkness is blinding her. You see it. But soon, you won't. I'll take you farther than the woods, where we belong."

Dread uncoiled in Constance's gut. She'd temporarily forgotten about their dark clinging to them. Visions of her decomposing face in the bathroom mirror returned to her. Her mother's flat voice, uninspired and emanating from somewhere else, somewhere empty. Mama had acted so strangely at dinner that night. That's when Constance noticed her shadow's depth and deformity for the first time.

"But she's not alone. There's an evil spirit in that house. Its roots run through its walls, down through the foundation to the sour earth. We're here because of that evil."

They'd reached the cemetery. Rows of tombstones welcomed them. Constance expected to see familiar specters standing on their respective graves. However, the cemetery stood in its usual macabre stillness.

"So, you're here to save us from an evil spirit?"

"Yes. But also, I'm dead because of her. As are you."

The cemetery pitched and yawed beneath her feet. "What do you mean? Who are you talking about?"

"Shadow Mother killed us."

Constance couldn't think clearly. Her thoughts collided as she grappled with what she heard and what she thought to be true.

"I didn't realize it then, but Shadow Mother had her hands on me for days leading up to my drowning. I saw it–*her*–in the house. She secretly spoke with me in my room the night she drowned me." Adeline walked past several plots and stopped between their mothers' graves.

"She kept me company, and it was magical, like a fairy tale, but a strange one. At first, she just visited me in my room after dinner each night. Then I noticed her *on me* throughout the day. In my shadow. A new darkness."

Constance listened intently. The more she heard, the more fear she held.

"I didn't mind because having her with me throughout the day comforted me. She looked after me."

Adeline reached down and touched her own tombstone. Seeing a child's ghost touch their own grave did something to Constance.

"She waited in my room the night I died. I found her sitting on my bed. I walked into the room and shut the door so my parents wouldn't hear us talking." Adeline paused. Her face twisted as she dug up the details. "She wore my mother's clothes. She looked just like her, except black streaks ran from her eyes down her cheeks." Adeline dragged her fingers down her cheeks to show Constance. "She convinced me to let her join me for a bath, just like my mother used to do when I was little. It made me feel special. So I said yes."

Constance silently wept. She couldn't help it. How could she? She was listening to a child describe their ultimate deception.

"She undressed me. I felt so warm, like I was standing in sunlight. Then we stepped into the tub. Her feet and legs turned black and disintegrated as they entered the water. I panicked, but she assured me we were okay. As we lowered into the tub, more of her became water and soon the tub was full of black water. She turned me around so I could lean back against her chest. She wrapped her arms around me. I felt so much love at that moment. We slid into the black water and that was it. Shadow Mother took me under."

Shadow Mother.

The shadow distorting her vision, the shadow her mother wore, the shadow clinging to the house. The spirit hid in the shadows they cast, the shadows they *held*. They wore her like a skin.

"Who is she? Why would she do this?"

"Only one person knows, and I think she's somewhere among us." Adeline turned, scanning the forest surrounding more than a century of their dead. "I just can't find her."

"Maybe she's crossed over."

"Maybe. But part of her is still here. I look for her every night."

Constance looked into the surrounding woods. The darkness teemed with spirits. The thought of finding a single entity among them felt immense.

"I hope she comes forward when the time is right." Adeline dropped her arm and flickered erratically in and out of being like a poorly transmitted television image.

"Hey. Are you okay?" Constance took one step forward. Her feet breached the burial site. A static sensation raced up her legs and spread into her abdomen.

"Something's wrong. Mother?" Adeline's eyes widened, then rolled into her head. Her small, semi-transparent body pitched forward with tremendous speed, crashed into her grave, and blew apart like smoke in a gust of wind.

She was gone.

Constance ran.

CHAPTER 24

ABIGAIL

Abigail shut and locked the bedroom door and shuffled to her closet with the towel pressed to her steadily bleeding wrist. She gasped for breath as she ripped a jersey shirt and jeans from the closet. She tossed the clothes on her bed and rifled through her underwear drawer for bottoms and socks. Grabbing an old crew sock, she fastened a makeshift bandage around her wrist and tied it by pulling one end with her left hand and the other with her teeth. Then she guided her injured arm through the shirt, trying her best to hold the cotton sleeve away from her makeshift bandage as it passed through. The sock wouldn't last long against the profuse bleeding, but it was easier to manage than a towel and would give her enough relief to finish dressing and get the hell out of the house.

A raucous crash in the family room at the other end of the house startled her as she pulled on the stone washed Jordache jeans. Heavy footsteps came down the hallway and stopped outside her room.

BANG BANG BANG

Someone pounded on her bedroom door. Abigail bit her lip to contain a scared whimper.

Go for the window.

BANG BANG BANG BANG BANG

Abigail scrambled around her bed and yanked the cord on the blinds. They climbed the window in a slanted ascent, one side higher than the other. She needed out.

Then what? Would she run? And if so, where to?

BANG

Something slammed against the window. Abigail cried out and reflexively fell back onto her bed with her injured arms raised to shield her face.

BANG BANG BANG BANG BANG

More fists pounded on the door.

BANG BANG BANG BANG BANG BANG

A battery of strikes rocked the window pane. Trapped with no way to escape, Abigail crawled off the mattress to the floor and shimmied under the bed. Her wrists burned warm and sticky in the dark. The batteries at her door and window increased to an incredible tempo, like rapid-fire weapons.

She had nowhere left to run, and no one left to run to. Everything had fallen apart.

Abigail sobbed, then screamed in desperation. Spittle flew from her mouth. Her hot breath rebounded from the bottom of the box spring back into her face.

"Just kill me already! Kill me!"

The fists stopped pounding.

A soft rustling like fallen leaves tumbling over each other replaced the pounding in the hall. The winter night outside her window resumed its soft silence. Abigail's fear flipped to rage.

"You want to kill me? Do it!" She yanked herself out from under the bed and crawled to her feet, stumbling toward the door. "Kill me!"

Abigail ripped the door open and stared in disbelief. Stacked in a bloody pile at her feet lay a mound of dying starlings, necks broken and wings mangled. The trail of bodies stretched down the hall. Smears of blood shaped like exaggerated commas dotted the walls. Abigail lifted her head, stepped over the pile, and walked down the hall. Small, hollow-boned bodies crunched under her feet. She pressed each step, grinding feathers and soft innards under her heels. She left the hall and entered the open family room. Feathers floated through the air to the furniture and carpeted floors. The front door stood open to her right.

TAP TAP TAP TAP

Abigail's wrist dripped on the floor beside her bare foot. She needed medical attention, but she wasn't interested in being saved tonight. She grabbed her keys from the hall table and walked through the open door, slamming it as hard as she could on the way out.

CHAPTER 25

CONSTANCE

"Mama!" Constance sprinted down the path to the house. The engorged moon followed her across the sky while spirits ran alongside her in the woods, yelping and mimicking her cries. Their energy spurred Constance on.

A sudden and unexpected encounter had pulled Adeline from her in the cemetery.

But which mother? Constance didn't know if Adeline had spoken of her mother, Lydia, or Shadow Mother, but she heard the surprise and desperation in her words. The girl sounded confident, but scared. Her warnings dug into Constance's consciousness, rooting there and sowing fear. The consequences of existing in the house with their mother any longer were greater than she'd previously thought. She had to protect Delilah until she crossed over.

If they survived one more night, she'd have time to prepare Abigail for their departure. She'd tell her sister everything she'd learned from Adeline in the morning. Abigail would understand. She'd want what's best for them. She'd see the point of living to honor them.

Constance just needed one more night.

The house and backyard filled her vision, but the landscape had shifted. She no longer saw the world beyond their property. Their yard along the sides and front of the house faded into a cold, empty chasm. The house, yard, and woods stood alone in a vast nothingness.

Constance bounded up the back porch steps in one fluid leap. She ran across the screened porch and through the back door.

"Mama!"

No answer.

The kitchen area appeared as it would any night of the week, illuminated only by the single kitchen sink light.

Go.

Constance rushed through the hall and looked upstairs without stopping. No light, no sound. She moved toward the foyer and its adjacent rooms.

Not the sitting room. Please.

Constance stopped hard a few feet from the archway to the sitting room. The foyer's floorboards rolled in shining black waves. Diamonds shimmered in the roiling pitch like glimmering stars in an inverted night sky. In one smooth motion, the diamonds turned and fixed on her.

Bird's eyes.

Starlings.

A moan slipped through her throat. "Please."

The congregation parted, granting her narrow passage into the foyer. Constance took a tentative step forward and judged their response. The flock remained docile and non-threatening. She took another step, and the flock parted further, allowing access to the archway. Constance leaned forward and peered around the corner into the sitting room.

"Mama."

Constance trembled. Delilah hovered above the center of the sitting room, arms outstretched like a crucified patroness, eyes closed, her naked body coated in starlings and rolling shadow. Layers of black and charcoal gray rolled from Delilah's body to the ceiling above, collecting like a thundercloud, then spilling into the corners and down to the floor.

The ravenous starlings feasted. They pecked and pulled the shadow as it wormed from Delilah's elevated body. Their small heads shook wildly, ripping black threads from the stream and swallowing them down like scraps of flesh.

Fluttering bodies clung to the walls and darted from corner to corner, their wings whipping wisps of black cloud into the air.

Constance stood rigid and terrified. Their time to cross over was past due.

A drop of liquid fell from the ceiling onto Constance's shoulder. Then another. She turned her head and saw her thickening shadow open like a mouth to accept the liquid as it fell. Constance screamed and swiped at her shoulder, whipping the shadow into a rolling wave. More liquid fell to her head and face. Her shadow fought to regain its layer.

Stumbling backward in disgust, she wiped her face and looked up for the liquid's source.

Black water spilled from a seam running down the center of the hall ceiling. Constance watched the seam expand to the full width of the foyer. Behind her, a murky stream cascaded down the steps in a babbling flow, spilling to the floor and running in all directions. The starlings whipped into a frenzy. Their dark blue bodies filled the air, shooting like plump arrows from room to room, snatching shadow and black water in frenetic bolts.

Constance crouched and covered her head.

"Mama!"

The starlings responded with manic cries. Constance covered her ears and screamed. She squeezed her eyes tight to protect them from the flying birds. Their beaks plucked at shadows on her ankles and calves, nipped at her thighs and arms, crawled across her back, and buried their faces in her hair.

A sudden realization ground her escalating panic to dust.

I'm already dead.

Until now, Constance hadn't fully grasped this reality. The process of coming to terms with her death seemed stunted and immature and now, while cowering in the foyer as a battle of will, fear, and the unknown unfolded in a blitzkrieg about her, she accepted her death and the power it gave.

Constance blasted up from the hoard and roared into the torrent of black water and flying birds. Starlings dodged her like a school of fish evading a predator. Anger blew through her, hot and metallic. She raged against every injustice, every terrifying dream, every crippling vision she'd endured.

Constance burst into flames and elevated from the floor. Relief overwhelmed her and confidence overtook her fear, unbridled and ready for war. Her fire lit the darkness, chasing the shadows from the ceiling and edges of the room. In the center of the room, Delilah hovered, coated in writhing starlings, her eyes closed and her mouth hanging open.

Constance sailed over the thrashing sea of birds, opened her arms, and embraced her mother.

Delilah's eyes shot open.

"Constance!" Her eyes took in the chaos unfolding around them.

Constance squeezed her mother. "We need to leave. Our time has come." She closed her eyes and imagined lifting her mother from the room. She tried to imagine them floating through the floor to the upstairs, but they didn't budge.

Delilah's shadow pressed hard against Constance's grip. The black water raining from the ceiling became a smothering deluge.

Delilah slipped in her hands.

"No!" Her flames grew.

Their shadows shrieked and writhed.

Now at arm's length, Delilah's face twisted into a deep sob in the light of her daughter's fire.

"I can't leave Abigail." Black tears fell from Delilah's eyes.

"But, *she's alive*. We can't have her now. Her time will come."

Shadow Mother crawled up Delilah's neck and chin and pried her fingers into her mouth.

"Mama!" Constance raged harder, forcing her flames higher and hotter. The light chased the shadows from Delilah's face. Her eyes grew wide in the intense glow.

"She's here."

Constance's stomach bottomed out. She groaned, her fingers slipping from her mother's arms. A dreamy smile filled Delilah's face.

"Abigail's here."

"Mama–" Blinding light stole Constance's vision as her arms flew open.

A familiar shape emerged in the light. Adeline's voice overcame the cacophony of flame and rain.

"It's time."

CHAPTER 26

ABIGAIL

Abigail's right wrist throbbed as she gripped the steering wheel in both hands. Although the bleeding seemed to slow, the makeshift sock bandage appeared mostly soaked through. Blood had run down her arm, saturated her shirt, and formed a circular stain on the thigh of her jeans. Abigail could do little about it unless she stopped at the hospital, but that was out of the question.

"That's a nasty gash you've got there," Steph said from the passenger seat. She rested one Converse-clad foot on the dash, and the other shoeless, mangled foot sat on the floorboard. She twirled her finger in her hair and chomped on an oversized wad of gum.

"You definitely need to see a doctor. Hospital's that way." She tipped her head to the passing crossroad.

"I'm not going to a hospital. I'm going home."

"Well, you may not make it there if that bleeding keeps up. You left quite the mess in the house. There's only so much juice to squeeze out of that aging body of yours, girl."

The Honda barreled down Route 60, leaving the lights of the expanding Williamsburg suburbs behind. She'd reach the Whispering House in fifteen minutes if she didn't encounter any night construction. Abigail thought they'd never finish widening the road, although she appreciated the project and the increased traffic it would bring to the store. Maybe they'd add a new exit to Interstate 64—

"Yo! Wake up. You'll get yourself killed nodding off like that," Steph said.

Abigail blinked her exhaustion away and steered the car to the center of the lane. She squirmed in her seat and sat up. She'd nodded off. Maybe she'd lost more blood than she realized.

"It's not too late to turn back and go to the hospital. You know Constance would tell you the same if she were here."

"If you're only here to keep me from my mother and sister, you may as well haul ass. I'm going."

"You must not be paying attention." Steph dropped her foot from the dash and leaned her open head over the center console. Abigail unintentionally recoiled. "I'm trying to help you. I tried to keep you from going home, didn't

I? I knew you'd hurt yourself. And I woke you up when you started nodding off. What more can I do?"

Abigail pressed the plastic turning signal arm down as she decelerated and stopped at Anderson's Corner.

"This is my stop," Steph said. She leaned toward Abigail and spoke plainly. "There's evil in that house. None of you are safe there. It's not too late to turn back. Please."

"I'll see you tomorrow," Abigail replied.

"No, you won't."

Abigail kept her eyes on the windshield and watched Steph cross the road ahead of the Honda. A truck blew through the intersection, barely missing the teen as she crossed the road. Not that it would have done any damage. Steph left the road, crossed the ditch, and entered the woods as a silhouette.

Green light.

Abigail rocketed the car through a gradual left turn in the intersection. Once she straightened the car, she glanced over her shoulder into the backseat to ensure she hadn't picked up any other unwanted passengers.

A nest of bees swarmed in her anxious belly when she thought about how close she was to the house. She cleared her throat and rubbed her eyes to wake herself and prepare for her arrival. Lifting her arm closer to her face, she inspected the bloody sock in the moonlight.

A dark blue streak flashed in her headlights and smashed into the windshield.

Abigail jumped in surprise. Her foot shifted from the gas pedal to the brake when another object struck the windshield. A red smear slid across the right half of the glass.

BAM BAM BAM

Starlings collided with the windshield in rapid succession. Abigail flinched as a star-shaped fracture exploded in the windshield, following the blinding barrage of bodies. Abigail lifted her foot off the gas and prepared to brake. She sensed the turn for The Whispering House ahead. She pressed her face to her side window and saw the house emerge from the treeline.

Abigail slammed the brakes and the Honda skidded across the frozen blacktop. She yanked the steering wheel hard left and bounced the car into the front yard. She threw the car door open and sprinted across the yard. Running partially blind, she shielded her face with her left arm and cradled her right against her body. Starlings zipped past her like compact missiles. The sound of Constance's distressed voice somewhere inside the house increased her urgency as she took the front steps two at a time and crashed into the front door.

She burst into the foyer and choked back a scream as black rain fell from the ceilings and poured down the walls in rivulets. The floor was alive, writhing and undulating in screeching waves. Starlings crawled over each other on the floor and snatched at the air in twitching, seizure-like movements. Others flew into walls and collided in midair in the torrential downpour of inky rain.

A bright flame illuminated the sitting room walls, its source out of sight from the front door.

Constance!

Abigail stumbled to the archway in time to see her mother and sister enveloped by a blinding flash of light. Behind her, starlings fled through the open front door in a solid column of dark blue feathers, the house vomiting them into the night sky.

As the light subsided, the darkness reclaimed the sitting room in the spaces between the cascading flow.

Her mother and sister were gone.

A series of slamming doors shook the house. The intense vibration temporarily jostled the persistent downpour.

Doors slamming upstairs. Water coming through the ceiling.

The tub.

"Connie!" Abigail spun in the pooling water and ran for the stairwell. Stray starlings dive-bombed her in the narrow hallway, pounding her arms and head with their mass. As she ran, the viscosity of the water at her feet thickened and became tacky, like a drying bed of blood beneath the running water. Memories of her shower and the unnatural sound the drain made as it consumed her blood flipped her stomach.

She grabbed the banister with her injured arm and winced against the resurgence of pain. Her head swam with the sudden change of direction, reminding her of the significant blood she'd lost. She regained her bearings and took the stairs two at a time.

The last step resembled the head of an active waterfall. A thick black stream of water cascaded from its edge, feeding dark effluent to the stairwell. The bathroom door stood closed a few feet away. Abigail closed the distance in two long, wet strides.

"Please don't leave me!"

Abigail reached for the doorknob when a hand shot from the solid wood and stopped her with sudden, brutal force. She no longer heard the water rushing around her feet and down the stairs behind her. The muscles in her arms and legs went rigid, wound tight and immovable like steel cables. A single, semi-transparent arm held her catatonic in the hall.

Adeline emerged from the closed door. Her eyes rolled down and into position when her form solidified.

"I'm sorry, Abi."

Abigail tried to speak, but her words came out as a soft, mashed blend of gibberish. Inside, she screamed, punched, clawed, and kicked. Inside, she raged.

"Your Mama's been here too long. But I can't let her take you. It's not your time."

Abigail stuttered, unable to speak through a jaw clenched so tight she feared her teeth would shatter under the pressure. She towered over her cousin's ghost, but it didn't matter. Adeline was far too strong.

Eyes wide and fierce, Abigail shook her head from side to side in protest. Adeline lifted her hand a few inches, and Abigail's body followed. Her heels left the river at her feet. Her toes dipped inward in the flow, trying to find the floor and regain their traction.

Adeline continued forward, driving Abigail through her open bedroom doorway across the hall. With one snappy flip of the wrist, Adeline shoved Abigail into the room. Her soaked sneakers squeaked across the bare hardwood floor as she lost her balance and stumbled backwards into the vacant room. Abigail's body went limp and collapsed to the floor. She reached toward her cousin with her bloody, injured wrist and fingers shaking uncontrollably.

"No! Wait! I can help—"

Adeline thrust her hands from right to left, slamming the door shut between them. Abigail scrambled to her feet and crashed into the door.

"Constance! Don't do this! Don't leave me here!"

Abigail pounded and pulled at the door, but nothing worked. Adeline had locked her in her room like a misbehaved child, forcing her into isolation against her will. Helpless and defeated, she sobbed with her head against the door, her hands fruitlessly working the immovable knob.

"Come, child." Deep, creamy, and foreign, a voice from the shadows behind her slithered into her ears and formed a block of ice around her racing heart.

Abigail instinctively remained perfectly still, facing the door. Her thoughts whipped into a frenzy of fight-or-flight images, but paralysis won. A surging tremble took hold of her nerves.

"Don't be afraid. I won't hurt you."

Abigail faced the dark expanse of the room. Moonlight, shrouded by a sheer curtain, pulsed in and out of the window across the room. To the left of the window, two eyes hovered in the center of a black mass in the corner. Slick fingers slid along her exposed arms to her injured wrists. Something like tiny mouths sucked on her wounds.

Abigail let them work, immobilized by fear and a strange sense of acceptance.

"I'm the mother you seek. The others abandoned you. I want eternity with you." Shadow Mother contracted and expanded along the wall, avoiding the moonbeams dancing on the worn hardwood floor.

"Who are you?" Abigail asked, barely able to hear her own voice over the static in her mind telling her to flee from this house and never return.

"They betrayed you," Shadow Mother said.

"No."

"*Yes*, they did. They chose death over you, didn't they? Your cousin locked you in here. You're unwanted, like I was unwanted." The moonlight flickered like a strobe light, then regained its rhythmic pulsing. "You tried to join your mother and sister. Isn't that right?"

"Yes." Abigail's will to fight slipped away. She was tired of sacrificing for everyone else. Their rejection hurt her. Her arms hung like lead weights at her sides, wrists throbbing. A new sensation bloomed in her wounds. The sucking mouths felt *good*. They scratched her itch, settled her hunger, eased her pain.

"They left you behind. Let me change that. Let me take you to them."

"Take me." Abigail gave herself over.

Strips of moonlight slid across the floor, pooled in the center of the room, then dimmed to nothing. As her vision fell into total darkness, Abigail let her fear go for the last time. Gradient waves of black and gray swirled in her eyes. Peace washed over her.

"I'll be your caretaker, your protector. I'll give you what you want, child."

A hand took hers in the dark and led her into the unseen. Abigail shed her identity with each step.

A familiar shape emerged from the depths of nothingness.

A worthy vessel to ferry her home.

A casket.

CHAPTER 27

CONSTANCE

"Mmmmmaaa!"

Constance beckoned her mother, but her mouth refused to move. She stood statuesque beside the sink in the pitch black bathroom. Directly across from her, Delilah kneeled beside the tub as she had earlier that day. Except now, the tub ran over, black water breaching its sides in a steady stream.

Constance's eyes slowly adjusted to the new darkness. She no longer burned, her flames arrested in transport. She wasn't sure how they'd arrived in the upstairs bathroom, but she suspected Adeline had something to do with it.

But why couldn't she speak? Why couldn't she move?

Delilah sat in a prayer position with her legs beneath her, hands pressed together as the water oozed like crude oil from the tub to her thighs. A swell of bubbles disturbed the rippling, silky surface of the water. Constance strained to see. Was Adeline coming to them again? Constance suddenly wished for nothing more in the world than to see her young cousin rise from that godforsaken water to liberate her from uncertainty and fear.

A face surfaced, bobbed momentarily, then sank rapidly. Constance tried to lean forward to identify the visitor, but she remained unable to see clearly in the near total darkness.

The thrashing began.

Delilah groaned, her face shaking but features frozen. Undeniable fear widened her eyes.

Two arms rocketed up from the water, fingers splayed and grasping, before finding the tub's curved lip. Curling, gripping, tendons and muscles stood at attention as they pulled their host from the black water.

Lydia Jones entered their world with a massive gasp.

She stood tall in the elevated tub, arms straight at her sides, head back, and spewed water from her open mouth.

Terror blitzed Constance in a rolling wave of convulsions. She tried to slam her eyes shut or run, but the force holding her squeezed harder. She pleaded instead.

"No no no."

Aunt Lydia's eyes opened as she lowered her head and found Constance. A loving smile crept across her dead aunt's lips.

"Oh, Connie–"

Movement on the floor caught Lydia's attention. She turned her head and saw her sister's upturned face. Tears streamed down Delilah's cheeks. Her hands remained clasped in prayer.

Lydia scrambled from the tub and embraced Delilah. After so many years of death and separation, their spirits finally reunited. Delilah's body went limp in her sister's arms. Constance wanted to tear Delilah from Lydia and protect her, but she was helpless and immobile, frozen in place by an invisible force.

"Delilah. I've been waiting for you."

Heat rose in Constance. She needed to protect her mother. She tried to move forward, to test her abilities again, and failed. As fast as her anger rose, her invisible captor suppressed it.

"She's safe. I won't hurt her," Lydia said, comforting Constance from across the room.

Constance didn't believe her, but what choice did she have? She had to relinquish concern and accept their situation. This was bigger than them. They were characters in a story she hadn't written.

"Speak sister." Lydia held Delilah at arm's length.

"I'm not ready," Delilah said. "Abigail needs us." Delilah looked at the closed door behind Constance.

"You *are* ready. We'll take care of Abigail." She cupped her sister's face in her hands. "It's time to come home. Your whole family is waiting for you." Lydia turned to Constance. "You too."

"Iiiii ..." Constance droned.

"You're both coming home," Lydia reinforced. Lydia had chosen words Delilah needed to hear. They'd never get her to crossover without Constance. And in her current state, they couldn't trust Delilah to return.

Constance stared hard at her mother's form and realized her shadow lacked hard edges. Her darkness filled the air around her but appeared barely perceivable in the unlit bathroom.

Constance closed her eyes and thought, *no light*.

She opened her eyes, and Lydia nodded to show her understanding. This had to happen in darkness. Delilah would not see her shadow and Constance would not see her reflection in the mirror or the shadow growing on her with each passing minute. They needed protection from themselves for this to work. They needed protection from Shadow Mother.

Movement rocked the tub behind Lydia.

A face. Gone.

Thrashing.

Lydia released Delilah, turned and held her arms out to her sides. Water ran from her burial dress and matted hair to join the rushing stream at their feet.

"Stay back."

The crown of Adeline's head broke the water's surface. Small hands reached up to their mother. Lydia bent forward, grabbed Adeline under the arms, and lifted her to her feet like a mother helping her child from a kiddie pool. Adeline stepped from the tub, wiped her wet hair from her face, and walked briskly toward Constance.

"Don't move," she said. Constance braced for contact.

Adeline raised one arm, put her head down, and stepped *through* Constance. A bouquet of vanilla, bubble gum, and embalming fluid filled Constance's nose.

Oh, Adeline.

A wave of nausea and heartbreak, brief and overwhelming, broke over Constance, followed by a strangely distinct sensation of having her strings cut from the puppeteer who'd controlled her since arriving in the bathroom. Her legs and arms went limp. She grabbed the sink to steady herself.

From the corner of her vision, she watched Adeline pass through the door.

Constance heard Abigail's distressed voice in the hall, despite the rushing water and the closed bathroom door. Free to move, she grabbed the doorknob, but it wouldn't budge. She closed her eyes and tried to step through the door as her cousin had, but she couldn't. She didn't know what to do.

"We need to help Abigail. We can't leave her out there."

"She can't be here when you crossover," Lydia said. "This is not for the living to experience."

"Well, I can't leave her like this. Not without saying goodbye." Constance's throat tightened as her emotions peaked. Now on the doorstep of crossing over, reality and panic set in. All the doubts she'd fought off until this point crashed into her.

She couldn't be dead. Her dead mother, aunt, and cousin couldn't be there. This cursed house couldn't possibly exist in a perpetual state of black water, shadow, and fire.

Where would they go when they finally crossed over? What waited for them on the other side? Would she find the peace of heaven or an eternity of continued torment?

The delicate membrane separating her confidence from fear ruptured, and she plummeted into a panic. The time to face her worst fear had come. She couldn't let go of her sister in this way.

Adeline had told her she could return to see Abigail again. But what if she'd lied to overcome Constance's resistance? What if she crossed over and discovered she couldn't come back?

Abigail screamed from somewhere close, but a slamming door cut her cry short.

"Abi!" Constance hammered the door with her fists.

"Adeline won't hurt her. She's here to protect her," Lydia said.

"How can you say that when you want to leave her in this house with Shadow Mother?" Constance imagined Abigail suspended in the sitting room as her mother had been, crawling in shadow and death. She recalled the spidery black fingers crawling up Delilah's neck and into her mouth.

She'll climb into Abigail and end her life. She'll take her from you forever.

"We leave through the flow," Lydia said. "We'll take your mother home, then we'll return to take care of the evil in this house."

"How? You've done nothing to defeat her so far. We don't even know who she is."

An energy circulated around Constance in the dark while Delilah rocked beside the tub.

"We're close to finding answers, Connie. You must trust me. But right now, taking your mother home is more important. She needs you."

Behind Constance, a breeze passed through the closed door, signaling Adeline's return to the dark bathroom. The girl moved quickly past Constance to her mother.

"We have to go. There isn't much time." Adeline said.

"Where's Abi? Is she okay?"

"She's not safe here. We need to ferry you across and immediately return."

"I'll stay. You two take my mother and I'll stay here with Abigail." Constance negotiated.

This time, Delilah spoke, "I'm not leaving without you, Connie. Let your sister be. She's a big girl." Her voice dropped an octave. "Besides, she'll have her day, just like we did."

Constance went cold. Her hands broke out in a clammy sweat and her feet grew restless beneath her.

"What are you thinking?" Constance tried to understand why her mother would suddenly accept to the proposition of leaving Abigail behind.

Delilah drew a big breath and sighed. "It's true. It's part of our bloodline. We never die old and we never die peacefully. Trauma defines us. It's your sister's birthright."

Constance couldn't believe her mother would so casually concede to Abigail's eventual death.

Lydia interjected. "Help me, Adeline. She doesn't have much longer. I'll take Delilah and you help your cousin."

Adeline gripped Constance's shoulders in the heavy darkness. "I promise you we'll come back. Okay?"

"Tell me what to do." Constance gave in. Her body shook uncontrollably. She'd never encountered a terror so tangible and disabling.

Adeline took her by the hands and led her to the tub. "We'll leave together, okay? Just follow me."

Adeline and Constance stepped into the tub and steadied their feet on the slick tub bottom. A calm settled on Constance moments away from her new existence. Adeline laced her fingers in Constance's and lowered herself into the water. Water swelled and spilled over the tub's sides as they displaced the black liquid around them. The water startled Constance as it pulled her in. Her bottom came to rest on the bottom of the overflowing tub. Adeline huddled closer and pressed her forehead to hers. From outside the tub, Lydia placed her hand on Constance and locked eyes with her.

"We'll follow you down."

"You're incredibly brave, Connie. I love you." Delilah swayed beside Lydia. Her eyes looked like two extinguished lights in the unbroken darkness.

"Are you ready?" Adeline asked.

Constance nodded, closed her eyes, and let the afterlife pull them under.

CHAPTER 28

ABIGAIL

The coffin lid made a sucking sound as she raised it with her right hand. The smell of hard water wafted up from the open box before a thick stream of water broke over the edge and ran onto her feet.

"The flow carries us home," the shadow said, much closer now but out of sight behind the open lid. "Enter the flow and drink deeply, for this is the water of life, the Blood of the everlasting darkness which pours out for the purpose of eternal life. Indulge in the flow to find relief, redemption, and the afterlife."

Amen, Abigail thought. Shadow Mother's words reflected the depth and gravity of a religious ceremony, dramatic, influential, and intoxicating. Abigail's spirit calmed at the edge of her frantic conscience. She kneeled beside the ornate box, dipped her hands into the lukewarm water, and pressed her arm to the bottom until her fingers found the silky cushion. A strange, erotic energy radiated up her arm and into her neck. An urge to feel that energy throughout her body bloomed in her core and transmitted into her spine. Abigail's limbs ached with the craving. Every cell begged for submersion.

Without removing her arm from the water, Abigail slowly lifted her opposite leg and lowered it into the casket, displacing more water from the container to the surrounding floor. Phosphorescence sparkled near the water's surface when she lowered the rest of her body into the liquid. She straightened her legs to their full length, her heels reaching their home at the end of the coffin. A foreign gravity urged her upper body into the water. She relaxed against the pull and lay all the way back. The casket's liquid load filled her ears and flooded her mind with barely discernible transmissions. The words strung together in an uninterrupted whisper.

... Succumb Release Commit Flow Reunion Acceptance Sacrifice Love Mine Bottomless Eternal Forest Internment...

Shadow Mother filled the ceiling above her, then dropped down to kiss the water. A shimmer radiated across the dark mass as it sipped Abigail's essence. Mother groaned, deeply pleased, and ready to feast. Floating flat on her back, Abigail drew shallow breaths and stared up into Mother's endlessness.

"Bring me to them." Her lips moved just above the surface, her voice muffled in her submerged ears.

Mother lowered into the water and joined her. The liquid grew viscous and hot around Abigail as she relinquished control and allowed Mother's weight to pull her down.

Full dark.

Abigail sat facing the woods at the edge of the cemetery, her small legs crisscrossed beneath her. Dandelion seeds drifted through a light, persistent breeze. She held one partially intact stalk in her hand. One slow twirl allowed the breeze to sweep the rest of the small white seeds into the air. She must have pulled it from the lawn. Dandelions were perfect summer flowers, in Abigail's opinion.

Was she outside to spend time by herself, or was she waiting for someone?

She waited. But she couldn't recall who she waited for or how she'd arrived in the yard. Everything seemed so sudden and mysterious, yet perfect.

"I don't remember much at all," she said in her dreamy young voice. She strained to put the pieces together. Her damp clothes stuck to her skin. That made little sense. It was warm, but not enough for her to sweat through her clothes. And her hair was wet, like she'd just bathed and not bothered to towel dry it before coming outside. Beads dropped from the ends of her hair to her soft, white cotton dress.

A dress? To play outside?

Home.

Summer.

"Connie ..."

The sound of footsteps on the path behind her caught her attention. She shielded her eyes from the harsh sunshine to see who approached.

Twenty feet away, Constance appeared on the path. Her drab, soaked clothes hung from her in stark contrast to the bright summer yard.

"Connie!"

Her sister turned, saw her, and ran as hard as Abigail had ever seen her run. Abigail sprang to her feet. She thought to run, but Constance closed the gap so quickly she braced for impact instead. Constance swept her into her arms and squeezed her so tight she thought she'd collapse a rib.

Constance held her at arm's length to look at her. Her eyes spilled tears of fear rather than joy.

"Why are you here? What did you do?"

Abigail sensed someone else with them. Her cousin Adeline emerged from behind Constance. Where had she come from? She hadn't seen her approach with Constance.

Constance grabbed her by the shoulders. "You shouldn't be here, Abi. What did you do?"

Abigail's tears came quick and hot. "I don't know what you're talking about. You're hurting me." She tried to pull her shoulders from Constance's grip, but her older sister was too strong.

"Do something, Adeline! She can't be here." Constance sounded frantic.

"She's not gone yet," Adeline said. "We're not crossed over yet, Connie. There's still time to save her."

"Save me from what? I don't want to go anywhere. This is ..."

This is home? Her mind failed to affix the last word to her thought. Or was this their cousin's home? She remembered living in the house. She played in the yard just beyond the path. Her bedroom at the top of the stairs was ... Adeline's and not hers?

Her world felt terribly disjointed.

"I know this is confusing," Constance said. "But we can't live there yet. It's infested by Shadow Mother. Adeline and I will fix that, but we need time. Once it's safe, you can live a real life there and we can stay with you. But you *must* stay alive, Abi."

Abigail nodded. She wanted that life, in that house, with her loved ones. But a very real fear stretched its limbs in her heart, causing her to doubt what she'd heard.

"You don't know that, Connie. You don't know how to make the house good again. How long will it take?"

"You're right. I don't know how, but we'll figure it out. Regardless, you can't be here with us, and you can't live in that house the way it is now. Adeline will take you back. Just promise me you'll do what she says and you won't come back here again. Promise me."

"Why can't I be here with you? Where's Mama?" She shook free of Constance's grip.

Constance looked anxiously over her shoulder to the walking path. "She'll be here any minute now. But you can't be here when she arrives." Constance shoved Abigail toward Adeline. "Take her now."

"I'm not going anywhere!" Abigail planted her feet and pulled away from Adeline with all her strength. As she spun, off balance and blinded by fear and desperation, she saw the ground behind her was not as it should be.

A partially dug grave disturbed the ground in the next designated plot. Its edges looked rough and deep, like a muddy wound. The odor of freshly exposed clay filled the air. The hole was too shallow to fill with a body and casket yet, the gravedigger's work still in progress.

Adeline steadied her and she regained her footing at the hole's edge. Abigail couldn't pull her eyes from the grave. It felt magnetic. Their faces now inches apart, Adeline spoke in a low voice.

"Not yet, Abi. It's not your time."

"Take her back, Adeline. They're almost here." Constance grabbed Abigail and hugged her so tightly Abigail couldn't get her arms up to return the hug.

"I'll come back for you. I love you."

"Let me stay. I want—"

Constance cut her words short with a tender kiss. "I'll see you soon."

Abigail's heart soared as her vision shattered into a thousand images of her sister's face. The images fell like autumn leaves.

She fell with them.

Into the grave?

Into life.

CHAPTER 29

ABIGAIL

Thrust upward, Abigail breached the surface and gasped for air. Her body craved oxygen, skin assaulted by needles. She opened her mouth to draw a breath, expecting her body to continue its trajectory from the water, but a force arrested her momentum and drove her back under. Water flooded her mouth as she slammed her jaw shut.

The thrashing began.

Abigail rolled, kicked, clawed and punched at the force holding her under. Memories of Adeline and Lydia breaching the tub cycled through her panicked mind, giving her hope of joining them in the unnatural return of the dead to the land of the living. Her hands found the lip of the tub, and with one jerky motion, Abigail pulled free of the suffocating space bordering life.

Cool air kissed her face as she drew the sweet breath of rebirth. She pulled herself over the lip of the tub and spilled onto the tile floor. Abigail lay there for a few minutes, regaining her strength and coughing up fluid with every exhale. She flattened her palms to the floor, pressed herself up to a seated position, and collapsed against the wall. She needed more time to gather her strength. Gradually, her pulse steadied and the full physical sensation of life returned to her. She inspected her wrists as best she could in the unlit bathroom. Her wounds throbbed but the bleeding had stopped, the makeshift bandages shed to the water at some point.

With life came fear. Abigail could barely see, but she had to make sure she was alone. Her eyes strained to search the corners and edges for Shadow Mother. Nothing.

The water had stopped flowing as well. Abigail pressed her damp hands to the floor and crawled several feet, feeling the dry surface but not believing. She'd expected to find standing water. Before she'd climbed into that coffin in her room, the upstairs floor resembled a river bed. Now, probing in the dark on her hands and knees, she found gritty, dry tile. Bits of dirt, hair, and general grime clung to her waterlogged hands. A river of flowing water would have cleansed the surface of loose debris. These dirty floors belonged in a poorly maintained building.

Abigail reached for the vanity and pulled herself to her feet. Squeezing her eyes shut, she found the light switch on the wall and toggled the nubby arm. The bulbs came alive on the other side of her closed eyelids. She raised her hand to shield her sensitive eyes and slowly opened them to see the room.

No standing water at her feet.

No Shadow Mother crawling the walls.

A crushing weight settled on her heart.

I'm alone.

No one followed her back. No one, good or bad, waited for her to return.

No one.

Abigail reached for the doorknob, hesitated while she listened for movement in the house, then opened the door. Light spilled from the bathroom into the hall, disclosing a drab, neglected home. The walls needed paint. The floors needed to be swept. No one had cared for this place in many years.

Somehow, finding the house safe and in need of love scared Abigail more than she understood. Shouldn't she be happy to find the house empty?

The weight on her heart increased, pulling the life from her muscles. Her adrenaline crashed. She shuffled her feet across the dusty hardwood floors to her childhood bedroom and stood in the open doorway. The coffin no longer sat where her bed should've been. The night sky filled the window, the moon calling her over to see the outside world for herself. She crossed the room and looked down at the yard below. Her parked car stood in the driveway donning a fresh coat of winter frost. The yard wore an identical coat, the hard ground frozen and waiting for the morning sun to share its warmth in a few hours.

Seeing the evidence of winter made her *feel* cold. She rubbed her chilly, wet arms and turned back to the room. No one had snuck in behind her while the scenery outside distracted her. The shadows hadn't built into a pool on the ceiling.

She went to her closet, opened the doors, and found an old sheet folded on the shelf above the clothes rack. She pulled it down, shook it out, wrapped herself in it, and nestled into the corner.

Heartbroken and shivering, she waited.

CHAPTER 30

CONSTANCE

The afterlife welcomed Constance in a way life never could. As a child, she'd heard stories about heaven. As a teenager, she'd read poetry and classics from T. S. Eliot, Edgar Allan Poe, C. S. Lewis, and Dante, which brought her closer to understanding. However, those stories read among the living failed to predict the beauty of the moment among the dead.

Constance didn't awaken to a chorus of singing angels, billowing clouds, or a savior's loving face. Instead, she awoke, laying flat on her back in the cemetery's grass above her grave, surrounded by loved ones.

"Welcome home, cousin." Adeline sat beside her in the grass, beaming with a radiance only children possess. She lifted her hand from Constance's chest and nodded toward something beside her.

Constance's fingers intertwined with someone to her right. She turned her head and locked dreamy eyes with her mother. Delilah's eyelids slowly floated up and down like a boat riding a swelling ocean.

"Mama," she whispered. Delilah's eyes cleared.

"Constance." Delilah smiled and pressed her face into her cheek. "I thought I'd lost you in the in-between. I saw you on the path, but then you were gone." She pulled her face back and looked past Constance.

"Sister!"

Constance turned back toward Adeline and found Aunt Lydia kneeling beside the girl. A broad smile full of beautiful teeth filled her flawless face.

"Welcome home, girls," Lydia said, nudging them with one hand. Uncle Wade's hand appeared on Lydia's shoulder a second before his face and upper body came into view behind her.

"You gonna lay there all day or what? You've got people here to see you."

"Uncle Wade!" Constance couldn't believe her eyes. Oddly, she'd become used to seeing her aunt and cousin on the other side, but seeing her uncle for the first time since his passing surprised her.

Delilah and Constance looked up and saw Aunt Jenny and Uncle Hank standing at their feet.

"Jenny!" Delilah's voice undulated as she took her sister's hand and stood. Constance took Uncle Hank's hand and did the same. The family embraced each other in a joyous bout of affection.

"You look amazing," Uncle Hank said, holding Constance at arm's length. "Your scars." He paused and looked her over. "They're gone."

Emotion bathed her soul, but the physical effects ceased to materialize. She may have collapsed, overwhelmed by the relief of knowing she'd finally arrived where she belonged, reconnected to the people who made her brief life beautiful. Rather, the joy of love and communion strengthened her and filled her soul with an indescribable contentment.

She was finally free. She'd finally found her home.

"We did it," Adeline said, holding one hand up for a high-five. Constance laughed and pressed her palm to the girl's before lacing their fingers and pulling Adeline into her body for a firm hug. She recalled the times her cousin's ghost had terrified her on the other side. Those memories became more distant with each passing second in this wonderful reunion.

"You're clean now," Adeline said. "No more shadows."

Constance held her arms out in the perfectly warm sunlight. The shadows were gone. She looked for traces clinging to her mother, but Delilah's shadow no longer existed. They'd left the darkness behind when they crossed over. Shadow Mother remained on the other side.

With Abigail.

The cemetery trees spun around her for a moment. She'd promised Abigail she'd return to protect her. Her sister needed her now more than ever. Constance grabbed Adeline by the arm.

"I need to go back."

Delilah pulled away from Aunt Jenny and focused her attention on Constance.

"You can't go back. It's too dangerous."

"But Abigail needs me." She implored Adeline. "What do I do to get back to her?"

"You shouldn't go alone," Lydia said. "Returning is not as harmless as you may think. That side has a magnetism that's hard to fight."

"What does that mean?" Constance asked, frustrated with her aunt's warning. Adeline answered.

"When you cross over, you can only stay so long before you forget you left this place. It tries to keep you. It's not magic, but it feels like it." Adeline's words made clear the danger she faced. Constance risked being trapped on the other side, not by a physical barrier, but by a condition of awareness.

"I'll go with her," Delilah said.

"No way," Lydia replied. "It's way too dangerous for you. We barely got you to crossover this time. You're too sensitive to that place. We may not get you back again."

Constance recognized the frustration in her mother's eyes. Her mother wanted to protect her children but was powerless to act.

"I don't want Constance going alone," Delilah countered.

"I'll take her," Adeline said. "We don't know why, but the magnetism doesn't really affect me."

Constance wondered if their youth protected them from the magnetism. Perhaps they were more resilient because they had less time immersed on that side? Although Constance and Delilah had spent nearly the same time with the living after their respective deaths, she didn't suffer as badly as her mother.

"Why don't you guys go with them?" Delilah asked Wade and Hank.

The men exchanged troubled looks with Lydia.

"We won't survive the house," Hank said.

Wade took a step back and put an arm around Lydia. "Men are completely powerless over whoever is haunting that house. She almost killed me while I was there." Lydia placed a hand on the center of Wade's chest.

"We think she's one of us," Lydia said. "We think she lived here and is in our family's line."

Lydia looked past Constance to the tombstones behind them.

"Come. I'll show you." Adeline took her hand. They walked past two rows of graves and stopped at the edge of the clearing. Adeline pointed to the oldest tombstone. The old marker was smaller than the rest and had an obvious defect. Its face contained no names or dates. Constance realized she'd never seen it before. How was that possible?

"Don't worry, you're not going crazy. This one doesn't exist on the other side," Adeline said.

"How did you know what I was thinking? Can you read my mind now or something?"

"No, I just saw the confusion on your face. It's the same look all of us had when we realized this grave isn't on the other side."

"Okay. That's a tremendous relief. So what's the story here?"

"We're not sure yet, but we think the answers are in the house." Abigail pointed down the path toward the house.

Constance grew hopeful. Maybe they could live together again in the place they loved if they figured out who haunted the Whispering House.

"Take me back," Constance said, more confident now than ever.

"I need to show you one more thing first." Adeline walked toward the woods. She stopped before entering the shady treeline and pointed.

"Here."

Constance's hands shot to her mouth to stifle a cry. A girl about the same age as Constance lay on her side in the fallen leaves and pine needles. She wore a mottled white nightgown, grass and mud soiling the lower half and blood staining the arms. A baby lay in her arms, swaddled in a dingy blanket, its face stained with its mother's blood.

"Why are they laying here like this? Why hasn't anyone helped them?" A dozen questions fought to escape Constance's mouth. She took a step toward the mother and child, but stopped. Somehow, she knew she shouldn't touch them. They weren't meant to be saved. "Who–"

"We don't know. But I think the house does."

Adeline's words left Constance speechless. Maybe this girl and her baby had something to do with the spirits haunting the house. Had they lived there once? If so, they were family. Someone on this side had to know who they were. Constance realized she hadn't seen their other deceased relatives in the cemetery since crossing over.

"Can we ask our older relatives if they know who she is?"

"That's part of the problem. They aren't here."

"What do you mean?" Constance asked. She didn't like the implications of Adeline's answer.

"None of us have seen them on this side. I think they're somewhere in there." Adeline pointed into the woods.

Constance closed her eyes and remembered the spirits yelping and running alongside her through the woods as she sprinted to the house to save her mother. Were they lost family members warning her?

"If they aren't in the woods, I think the house has them." Adeline said.

The woods around the Whispering House swayed in a steady breeze, as if agreeing with Adeline.

Constance looked down at the girl cradling her baby in the woods and thought of the years of pain and trauma their family had endured because of the curse on their blood.

First, it killed Adeline. Then it manipulated Lydia and came for Constance. Their blood hadn't been enough. The house wanted more.

Now, only Abigail remained alive. And they'd sent her back to that dark hell to save her life.

Our blood wasn't enough.

Constance turned away from the girl in the woods. "Take me to Abigail. Take me back to the house."

WHAT'S NEXT?

The final novel of the series, *Banish the Dead*, becomes available in early 2025.

Join the list at https://www.lucasmarinowrites.com / for early access to new publications, exclusive content, and news. I'll never share or sell your information, and I'll never spam your inbox.

QUICK FAVOR

Thank you so much for dedicating your time to reading this book! May I ask a quick favor?

Will you please take a moment to leave a review on Amazon, Goodreads, or wherever you purchased the book? Your words have power. Your review can help this book serve more people. I appreciate you!

THOUGHTS AND THANKS

We made it through the second novel, kids! Thank YOU for reading this book. Hopefully, you're enjoying the series. I've written every word for you and you alone. Your constant support motivates me to be a better writer and bookseller. Let's keep this party going, shall we?

Of course, none of his would be possible without the support of my wife, Tammie. Dear reader, I cannot express in words how much Tammie suffered for you. She endured months of my questions, thoughts, plot rants, "Oh! I have an idea!" moments, and shared drafts. All jokes aside, thank you for being my daily sounding board, Tammie. I love you. Bring on the JB videos.

Caleb, Gabriel, and Madelyn – without you, I'd have no heart for writing. Thank you for the color and depth you give to my life.

Mom and Dad – thanks for cutting the grass at the lake while I hid away to write all the books this year. We can't wait to spend a day near the water with you!

A top team of professionals supported this novel, starting with my friend, book coach, and editor, Zach Bohannon. Thanks for the constant guidance, Zach. Working with you on this series is a blessing. I hope you enjoy reading a print copy of this book between drafts of our Only Darkness Remains series! (hint-hint, reader)

Clarrisa Yeo is the talent behind this amazing book cover. Clarrisa, you knocked another one out of the park! Thank you so much for making this series shine. Your covers catch eyes. I'm grateful for the art you share with me.

To my mentor and dear friend, Honorée Corder, thank you for the consistent optimism and morning conversations. You deserve a medal for listening to me every morning before coffee.

Finally, I extend my sincere thanks to the friends and readers following this series via my email newsletters. If you stuck around long enough to read this and you're finding out about the newsletter for the first time, join us at www.lucasmarinowrites.com ! We can exchange emails like pen pals.

MUSICAL INSPIRATION

- David Gilmour (with Romany Gilmour) - Between Two Points
  This one was my top listen while writing this book. Be still my nerd musician heart.

- Tesseract - Hexes

- Tesseract - Tourniquet

- Tesseract - War of Being (album of the year in this guy's opinion) (listen to Tender and Sacrifice ... stunning!)

- The Fixx - Saved by Zero

- Veil of Maya - Red Fur

- Opeth - Damnation (album)

- Deftones - You've Seen the Butcher

- Leprous - Melodies of Atonement (album)

- Monuments - Cardinal Red

- Flyleaf - Broken Wings

- Periphery - Only Smiles

- Periphery - The Way the News Goes

- Periphery - Wag Wings

- Periphery - Flatline

- Radiohead - How to Disappear Completely

- Radiohead - Everything in its Right Place

- Peter Gabriel - Love Can Heal (Dark Side Mix)

- Tears for Fears - Woman in Chains

- Spiritbox - Blessed Be

- Spiritbox - Circle With Me (check out the live performance with Tatiana "Tati" Shmayluk)

- Sevendust - Trust

- Sevendust - Ugly

Coming in early 2025 – *Banish the Dead*

The final novel in The Haunting of the Whispering House series

Available in paperback, eBook, and audiobook.

ABOUT THE AUTHOR

Lucas writes thriller, suspense, and horror fiction. If he's not writing, he's reading, playing guitar, or enjoying time with his family. Lucas is also the host of *The Suspense is Killing Me* podcast and cofounder of Sobelo Books, an indie publisher of dark speculative fiction.

A military engineer by experience, he spent twenty-one years in the United States Coast Guard. He earned his Doctor of Engineering and Master of Science degrees in Engineering Management and Systems Engineering at The George Washington University.

He now lives in a pile of trees in Virginia.